AGENT PHOENIX

Christopher Michael Carter

Supposed Crimes LLC • Matthews, North Carolina

This book is a work of fiction. Names, characters, places, and incidents are products of the author's imagination or are used fictitiously. Any resemblance to actual events or locales or persons, living or dead, is entirely coincidental.

Published in the United States.

ISBN: 978-1-952150-00-5

www.supposedcrimes.com

This book is typeset in Goudy Old Style.

CARBINE CITY. The street vendors worked diligently, selling potent steam cigarettes as well as assorted candy, and contraceptives that cloak when fitted. The young boy who ran the magazine and newspaper stand worked the passing crowds as he sold the latest SD cards of news and celebrity gossip. Members of society moved amongst each other with little interaction beyond a nod and a smile. The current of bodies flowed on the two-lane sidewalk; one for the able-bodied and one for citizens confined to hover-chairs, though many in a hurry used said lane for passing and getting ahead of the crowd. Neon signs were bright even under the golden sun of the day as were the holographic advertisements protruding from business establishments.

People stopped when the ground began to rumble. It was too early for the semi-annual earthquake simulation. The vibrations came on stronger as everyone looked at each other wondering what it was. The holograms flickered. The street vendors tried to stabilize their machines while the newsboy struggled keeping his cards from scattering about. Strangers held onto one another. The quakes were intensifying.

A manhole cover burst up into the air with a deafening *pop* before smashing through the windshield of a nearby vehicle. The trembling dissipated, eventually ceasing, but the people screamed and pointed to the area.

A smoky mist rose from the hole in the street, now sporting

cracks around its perimeter. Slight aftershocks pulsed. A big pair of hands gripped the edge of the hole as the man known as *The Feeder* ascended to the street. Large and donning a makeshift mech-suit - from the titanium-plated boots on his feet to the miniature satellite-laden helmet on his head – he smiled at the fear around him. In one of the gauntlets he wore was the handle to a weighty trunk, a yellow-green casing that pulsed with energy within its metal framing. The Feeder grinned and set it down to a loud thump.

"If you wish to run and scream, you may do so." His voice was mechanized and boomed outward to every ear in the vicinity.

While some civilians stood flabbergasted, others exclaimed in fear. Some hurried and left while others remained glued to their stance. The streets were crowding with people being trampled in the attempted escape. With each rise of volume of the commotion, the casing pulsated and throbbed. Another smirk from The Feeder and he leaned down to unlatch the device. A collective flinch and the crowd jumped back as the box opened. Hearts pounded and minds raced as to what would come next.

The rumble shook the ground once more before great tentacles shot forth, baring the same yellow-green shade along with metal wiring throughout. Two started from the case but more followed soon after, thick and growing by the second. Citizens ran but wouldn't get far before being grabbed by the slithery limbs. People shouted and pointed as the unlucky ones were dragged screaming into the box. After the first few bodies were collected, a bubble swelled from within the case. The Feeder watched in ecstasy as people were being taken by two, by three, by seven. The screams of those taken, along with witnesses, actually managed to drown out the usual city noise. Vehicles collided and buildings were taking a lashing, still beneath the volume of the chaos.

The Feeder's laughter was well-heard, however, as he stood amidst the pandemonium, unscathed. The small satellites on his helmet pulsed, emitting the vision of a hot sidewalk, but remained quiet. The Feeder's eyes throbbed in unison with the satellites. Citizens were grabbed by their arms and legs while trying to run. They kicked and screamed while dragged. Children were snatched from their parents' arms.

Meanwhile, the bubble continued to stretch and grow with each new addition. From vibrating and trembling to violently shaking, more and more tentacles quickly burst from within. In its fast growth, the bubble hardened, with its new shell reflecting The

Feeder to its right. The more people were taken, the more limbs shot forth. He listened to the cries for help and breathed in deeply with an unbreakable smile.

The federal craft sped down the streets with ease, dodging those who managed to run *that* far. The people saw that help had arrived and did their best to clear a path for the vehicle. Its exterior was slick and curved, aerodynamic, its coloring of thick single red, white, and blue stripes. Lights and holograms reflected off of its body, briefly printed with marketing. Inside, behind the black windows, the gloves gripped the wheel, the foot pressed and the engine revved. The driver cracked his neck but never moved his eyes from his target, a foe he'd faced plenty of times before.

"Be careful with this one. He's not like the petty crooks you're used to." The driver said to his new partner beside him.

"Copy that, Agent." Agent Martinie replied.

The driver turned swiftly and gave him a nod before coming upon the multi-limbed sphere, and the man feeding it. The cruiser came to a dead-stop, pushing air around it and sweeping assorted debris, before ejecting both men from the sides. Agent Martinie was still getting used to it and stumbled slightly, unlike his partner who landed solidly and had already drawn his weapon.

"Agent Phoenix..." The Feeder's voice boomed, audibly rippled. "We've been so hungry for you. This must be your new partner, how does *he* taste?"

AGENT PHOENIX – tall, athletic build, black hair – squared up and grit his teeth and snarled his lip. The uniform these men wore was black with chrome buckles and zippers. His boots stood firm, defiantly.

"How many times do I have to do this before you learn? This never ends well for you."

"Things change, Agent. Things change." The Feeder laughed.

Agent Phoenix noticed the new addition to his opponent's helmet, the satellites. He looked at the chaos around him, thinking, while his partner looked dumbfounded by the waves of tentacles and the damage they were causing.

"Martinie!" Phoenix yelled.

Agent Martinie snapped out of it quickly, drew his weapon, and began firing at the whipping limbs.

"Avoid hitting people, shoot *in!*" Agent Phoenix instructed as he walked closer to the center of the commotion.

The tentacles whipped and grabbed at the agents who fended them off with blasts. They dodged the lashing, ducking and rolling out of the way. The agents kicked and shot at the thick limbs from the orb in the case. Throughout the battle, Agent Phoenix kept eyeing the helmet radiating energy. Agents Phoenix and Martinie moved in closer together, firing at The Feeder's grabbers causing them to drop people on their way to the orb.

"Cover me!" Agent Phoenix ordered.

Agent Martinie followed suit, sending laser blasts from his pistol to the lively lashing yellow-green cords. The Feeder stood confident as his orb grew more powerful.

"You've finally met your match, Agent Phoenix." The villain grinned.

"Not today, Feeder. Not *you*."

The Feeder laughed while the mayhem around them raged on. The people screamed for their lives and the orb rumbled. The Feeder watched in amusement as Agent Phoenix shot at the orb inflicting minimal damage. To the large man's surprise, Agent Phoenix quickly turned and fired his pulsing laser above and around the Feeder's helmet, grazing the mini satellites. The transmission going off was interrupted and soon the satellites shattered.

"What!? NO!" The Feeder screamed.

The orb trembled and the tentacles dropped, lifeless. Upon hitting the street, each enormous snake-like limb became a person taken into the orb, which continued to gyrate before shrinking down. The tentacles were no more as the thick sheathing became gelatinous goop. Everyone now freed were soaked in vibrant fluids. Some of those who found themselves on the ground weren't present this morning but had been taken some time before. When they were done coughing up the thick liquid, they looked around, confused. Agent Martinie rushed to the aid of the discombobulated civilians while Agent Phoenix instantly moved to the now harmless Feeder with his weapon poised.

"It's over, Feeder. Your beast didn't work before and it's not working now even with your new controls."

The Agent's opponent looked at his broken helmet in bewilderment. The orb had shrunk back down to the bubble it was before and soon was no longer visible in the trunk. The Feeder grew angrier as the Agent approached him. A barrel extended from his gauntlet and he pointed at Agent Phoenix, dead in his sights, but was blasted in a flash of light, breaking from his arm in a cloud of sparks. Phoenix looked over to see his partner with his pistol pointed in that direction. The agents nodded to one another before moving in on The Feeder. Martinie kept his aim on the large man while Phoenix removed a rod from his boot. Agent Phoenix put The Feeder's hands behind him and placed the rod to his hands. Pressing the button in the center, the rod quickly bent and tightly gripped around the now-powerless man's wrists.

"Assess the situation, Martinie. I'm taking this one in."

"Yes sir." His partner said, before tending to the people gripped with fear and confusion.

"You ever get tired of lockup, Feeder?"

"I only grow tired of you, Phoenix. You'll get yours." He said being placed into the cruiser.

"Don't *feed* me that. I've heard it all before..."

CHRISTOPHER MICHAEL CARTER'S

AGENT PHOENIX

The Nightmare Returns

AGENT PHOENIX took his jacket off upon entering the locker room. Other agents were at their lockers dressing down to gym shorts and tanktops; some were back in uniform and leaving.

"Phoenix." They greeted.

"Hey guys."

"Good job this morning."

"Thanks. Just comin' in for a quick workout before going back out."

Phoenix walked through to his locker. On the inside of the door was a picture of he and his husband, Victor Louis-Phoenix, with the sun setting behind them. Victor was biracial, thin with short hair and glasses, and less than a year younger than Tobin, the decorated Agent Phoenix.

His shorts and shirt were removed and set beside him on the bench before hanging up his jacket. He stripped out of his uniform. First his boots, along with any weaponry attached. Next, his holster and pistol were hung up. He unbuckled his belt and undid his pants before sliding out of them revealing equally black boxers. His tight black t-shirt was pulled off, showing his muscular body and more than a few battle scars. After dressing in the standard gym clothes issued to all agents, he strapped on his tennis shoes and headed out.

The weight room was vast with state of the art equipment. Phoenix greeted the others and stepped up to the weights. He started with bicep curls. His muscles pumped in the warm-up.

When he was finished, he moved on to the chest press. He worked his pecs hard like he did everything else. Soon he was on lat pulls and then rows. Agent Phoenix worked his way around the room, hitting as many stations as possible in short high intensity bursts. He'd alternate with colleagues as they upped the weight to out-lift one another. Sweat, testosterone, grunts, laughter; his workout was finished and it was time to hit the showers and return to the office.

The offices of the Carbine City Agency were alive with worker bees trekking to and fro with assignments. Workers manned the telecoms, taking down information, occasionally assessing situations via holographic images of the caller's predicament. The wall, a screen stretching across the office, displayed the daily total of cases solved and those still open. The listing of criminals was color-coded to the degree of danger involved. Until this morning, The Feeder was at a rich orange; of course, now it was dimmed with his capture.

Coffee flowed. Delivered cubical to cubical to the call receivers trying to sort the info given to match the right field agent for the job. Each and every telecommunications agent underwent strict brackets of training, matching laws to agents and their specialties, so they knew very well how to spot what was needed. Few agents stood around the water cooler to share tips and stories. An assignment for everyone, and every agent for at least one assignment. Moving past the constant stream of numbers and blinking lights stood an office, enclosed behind thick layers of glass, and soundproof so distraction is at a low. Tobin Phoenix was in his office on a personal assignment.

"I was thinking the Cancun trip would be better. Get out in the sun. Have some drinks." Tobin spoke into the phone.

"I don't know. It sounds fun but it doesn't sound relaxing. A cabin in Colorado would be just the two of us. Just snowy-mountains-and-chill." Victor responded.

"I'm trying to help you out of your shell, out of your comfort zone."

"We need to get you out of *your* comfort zone. Cannon fights with monsters and madmen in the street? Yeah, I saw the news..." The tone in his husband's voice was clear.

"Babe, it's part of the job." The agent shrugged.

"I know. And it's this job that's keeping you from relaxing with me."

He looked at the phone. Victor wasn't wrong and that irritated Tobin all the more.

"Victor, I do this for you, for us, to keep you safe."

"Honey, I get that and I'm proud of you and I appreciate your services, but I'm tired of playing bridesmaid to these *things* you have to chase down."

"I'm trying to take you away from all of it for a little while. Out of the country. Beyond my jurisdiction and reason for action."

"And the moment Cancun has their own villainous problems, you'll step up because that's who you are. And I love that about you, I just want you to be able to turn it off. So a Colorado cabin with all source units shut off. Just us. No high speed chases. No nutcases in cybersuits. No metacreature hybrids."

Agent Martinie entered with something in his hand and something on his mind. Tobin turned to him.

"Hold on. Martinie's here. Let's ask him." He turned to his colleague. "Martinie, what would you choose for a getaway: a cabin in Colorado or a beach resort in Cancun?"

He was stumped, not expecting such a question.

"Uh, I don't know. Are you going for party and fun or romance and relaxation?"

"Huh..." Now Tobin was stumped. Which did the couple require most?

"Mm!" Victor grunted, hearing his husband's baffling.

"Yeah, yeah." He told him.

"Agent Phoenix." Agent Martinie urged.

Tobin knew that look.

"Babe, I gotta go. We'll talk about it more when I get home."

"Alright. Go save the world. I love you." Victor said.

Martinie opened his hand revealing a holopod.

"Love you too." Tobin said nearly absent while his eyes were glued to the pod.

The hologram popped up and flickered briefly before the image was crystal clear as Agent Phoenix hung up the phone.

Assorted men in similar coveralls - torn, ripped, and re-stitched over time - lined bank tellers and customers up side by side. Every person not in the tattered uniform shivered on their knees in the lobby of the bank. They struggled, fearing for their lives. Some crying, murmuring amongst themselves with others wincing hard in silence, trying to wish themselves out of the situation. A man entered the picture, short and stocky in an altered version of the coveralls - armored shoulders while sleeveless, revealing metallic tattoos reflecting light from the bright signs around them.

Agent Phoenix's eyes widened upon his entrance.

"Baxter..."

"This was at the Second National Bank." Martinie informed him.

The man stepped slowly and deliberately, eyeing each in the line. He walked behind them before motioning to his crew with a snap. They brought him an apparatus under a burlap cloth. Removing the covering unveiled a cannon of sorts. The machine's summoner hoisted the weapon with both hands, showing its weight, before placing his right arm deep inside. It locked in with a loud click.

"I was never a good student... But you'd be amazed how much I love to learn." He said in a low grumbling voice, viewing his choices.

His selection, a platter of minds, quivered. The machine powered up with an audible whirring. The kneelers flinched. The barrel pressed against a woman's head. Tears flowed as Baxter squeezed his fist. Power surged through the weapon from the back of the machine to her head. Her whimpering stopped in a jerk of her head. Her eyes stared blankly before her mouth dropped open. A thread of light darted up the machine. Baxter pulled it back, dropping the teller to the floor. The lineup screamed, flinched, jerked, and soiled themselves. The backend of the weapon opened up, ejecting a capped, glass vial of a milky neon liquid. After holding it up and looking at it, he threw it to one of his men, and stepped over to the next and continued.

While the agents watched, Martinie was confused and unnerved. Phoenix's eyes stayed glued on the leader of the ragtag group.

The assailants finished with the last in line and collected the vials, placing them all in an armor-plated briefcase. The bodies lay about, motionless with their eyes staring out at nothing for comprehension, while Baxter and his crew gathered their equipment without a hint of remorse.

"C'mon, boys, the chopper should be on the roof by now."

His thugs toted large bags of cash, along with other assorted valuables, and left.

Agent Martinie closed the hologram. Phoenix turned and moved to his desk. He could tell that his partner was curious. New to the Agency, Martinie simply saw the man as another crazy they'd have to take down but, from Phoenix's reaction, Martinie had an inkling there was something more.

"All right. Listen up."

Agent Phoenix walked over to his charging rack and removed two clips; one he loaded his pistol with and the other went in the pouch beside his holster. He returned to the desk.

"Baxter Combs, atop of our list," he pointed out of the window to the digital wall and Baxter's name highlighted in deep red, "He's out of hiding and back at it. His M.O. appears to remain the same - the consciousness of others."

He held out his hand and Martinie placed the holopod in it. Phoenix linked it to his desk and ignited a much larger hologram. It blew up to the center of the room, featuring Baxter and his weapon and goons, before Agent Phoenix magnified the view of the apparatus.

"Until the trail went cold, he was using this device to steal the energy, the memories, and life force of innocent civilians."

"Sir," Martinie took his eyes away from the weapon and looked over to him, "What does he do with them all?"

"He ravages through their knowledge for information - bank codes, passwords, etc. - and sells them. The money from the bank is an extra; chump change compared to what he would get for the information stolen. But knowing Combs, if he's hit one bank, he won't stop there. We need to get to him before he dissects and sells what he has, and before he collects any more."

Martinie looked at the holographic Baxter Combs. The man's hair was buzzed short but the light still reflected off of the metallic tattoos on his scalp, matching those on his arms. The look in his eyes was murderous, savage; while his visage appeared feral, he acted much more methodical. The image of Baxter burned into Martinie's mind. For some reason, a reason he couldn't put his finger on, this man seemed worse than The Feeder. The hologram closed abruptly.

"Let's hit it."

Agent Phoenix grabbed his jacket off of the rack and zipped it up and checked his pistol. He and Martinie left the office. Phoenix got everyone's attention and they put whatever they were doing on hold as he quickly summed up the situation. Most present remembered past reigns of terror at the hand of Combs. Phoenix and Martinie exited as a handful of agents followed suit to get to their cruisers. Office workers scrambled to pinpoint Baxter's location, sorting through various surveillance footage.

The two agents got in Phoenix's craft. He started it up as his monitor illuminated and he checked his fuel gage; they were set.

"Where to first?" Agent Martinie asked, fastening in.

"We'll hit the Second National Bank first and then off to find Baxter."

"So, those people, they're..."

"Dead? No. They're still alive, just in a vegetative state."

"What, they're in a coma? Braindead?"

"They'll be fine with their bodies in a safe place until we can return their consciousness."

The cruiser ran smooth. Agent Martinie watched Carbine City pass him at high speed while his partner drove. His precision revealed the amount of time on the job spent behind the wheel.

"And if their life-force isn't returned to them?" A skeptical Martinie asked.

"That's a scenario we're trying to avoid..."

Agent Phoenix gripped the wheel. While his eyes looked forward with sharpness, his mind reversed.

A series of memories flashed before his eyes like a clip reel in double time. Baxter Combs was the problem of the police before Phoenix and the Agency got involved. Multiple counts of murder, armed robbery, including banks and jewelry stores, and countless assault charges. He was rarely caught, evading the police and escaping the local cells he was placed in. When he came on the crime scene, Baxter was a thug with sharp objects in torn clothes. With a motto of 'Trust No One' he killed most of those unfortunate to work a job with him. He stepped up from low rent hood to playing with the big boys when he emerged with the weapon.

"Nobody knows where he got it, if he made it, or what." Agent Phoenix felt the need to explain. "He's not a hired gun. He doesn't take orders. Baxter works on his own accord and finds the highest bidder. Don't let his gang of goons fool you, he's a lone wolf."

Agent Martinie took that in and kept questions that would very well annoy his superior to himself.

Phoenix's memories continued. The first Baxter Combs case Agent Phoenix was pulled into saw him investigating a nursing home full of comatose cases, patients and employees alike. It wasn't until a plane was found in a hanger with the same situation that a pattern was noticed. While security footage was destroyed, the black box described the man and his apparatus along with his seemingly faceless crew; a temporary who's who of common hoodrats easily persuaded. The police were at a loss as to what the strange phenomenon could be.

He was bald back then, not counting the silver streaks throughout his scalp. When he became a new class with his machine the odd tattoos came with it. Whether or not there was a correlation between the soul stealer and the metal ink work, Agent Phoenix never found out but it always stuck out to him. Looking over the photos and file of Combs before and after his change, Phoenix could spot the difference and not just aesthetically. Baxter had a new ferocity about him.

During their battles Baxter Combs had proven to be Agent Phoenix's white whale.

The last time their paths crossed was almost a year prior to the current race against the clock. At the docks, Baxter had just acquired the last for his collection for the night when two of his followers were shot down. Baxter turned upon hearing the blasts and the bodies dropping as a result to find Phoenix with his pistol aimed. The thugs were stunned, unconscious but alive.

"It's over. Drop the case and put your hands up." Agent Phoenix ordered on the Carbine City pier.

"Just can't let me go, huh, Phoenix? When are you gonna drop it? You'll never get me, Agent, and I think you know this." Combs replied.

The man with the case in his hand never left the sights of the agent's gun.

"There's nowhere to run anymore. It's done. You're coming with me."

"You know," Baxter chuckled, "If our time together has taught me anything it's to always have a contingency plan."

The beeping below caught the agent's attention. Barrel still pointed at his perp, he looked down to see button-size lights on the back of the collars of the two henchmen he'd just dispatched of. The beeping sped up to a rapid pace and Phoenix knew it was nothing good. Baxter laughed and dove off the side of the pier to the dark water below as the bombs he placed on his men detonated. The bombs eviscerated the two men and tore the pier apart. Phoenix jumped but the explosion threw him further out. Deep in the black waters, he checked to make sure his limbs were intact. When he swam to the surface he saw the flames and smoke but no sign of Combs. The Agency searched and tracked but there were no more leads nor clues. Since that night Baxter had been a ghost, a bad dream, and now, the nightmare had returned.

"The bank's up ahead." Agent Phoenix said with their location in his sights.

"Looks like the local boys got there first." Agent Martinie added.

"We need to get in there before they muck it up."

They parked just outside the police tape marking off the bank. The flashing lights atop the squad cars painted the surroundings intermittently in red and blue. The Agency cruiser carried no flashing lights as its siren and image did the job of announcing itself. The agents exited the vehicle without the need of ejection. As they approached to cross the yellow tape they were stopped by an officer.

"No press." He saw their attire and their Agency craft. Another cruiser with two more agents arrived behind them. "Oh, it's you guys. Alright..." he reluctantly stated.

In no need of his clearance or invite, the agents moved past the lawman. When they entered, Agent Phoenix saw the familiar sight of a comatose crowd. The police hadn't been there long as they investigated the scene, stepping around the bodies. Phoenix looked over to his fellow agents and motioned out.

"Got here before the EMTs."

"They've been involved with a crisis." One of the colleagues informed.

An officer saw the agents and stepped over the bodies to get to them.

"Captain Conroy. This is my crime scene. They didn't tell me you all would be here." He told them in surprise.

"Well, we are here, so as of this moment this is a Carbine City Agency crime scene." Agent Phoenix told him.

He led the other agents past the cop, who followed behind. Phoenix kneeled down to get a closer look at the bodies.

"I just don't see this as a job for agents. We don't even know what happened yet." The irritated policeman said.

Agent Phoenix examined the back of their heads, seeing the same puncture wound on each. The vision of the security hologram played out before him and the weapon that made such odd marks.

"Yes, *we* do. Captain, please take your men and vacate the premises. We have work to do." Phoenix responded before leaning down close to listen to the breathing and heartbeat of the victims.

Captain Conroy did just that.

"C'mon, boys, let's go. Not our crime scene anymore."

They eyed the agents but didn't say anything and left. Agent Phoenix paid them no attention and looked up at the pair that came separate.

"You guys call this in and get them to safety. We have to leave *now*." Phoenix said, standing and turning to Martinie.

"Where to?"

"Baxter." He answered and the two left the others to take care of the victims.

They got into Phoenix's cruiser and fastened themselves in.

"How do we find him?"

"Just follow the green paper trail. Follow the banks."

The cruiser sped forth, passing the leaving cops.

"Guess we got there in time." Martinie said, looking out the window.

Phoenix pressed the center control panel on the dash.

"Nearest bank to Second National Bank."

"Carbine City Credit Union, one mile north on the corner of Baltic and Harper." The mechanical voice answered.

"We got you this time, you bastard."

The Agency craft picked up speed.

A helicopter flew over the busy city. Baxter looked down at all the bright holograms and the money they represented. His eyes lit up at the prospect and possibilities.

"Boys, I think we may step up from the bank scene. Just hit a few more and we'll be set."

His crew didn't respond beyond a "Yeah, boss."

Combs grew more excited seeing all the businesses, thinking of the information he could attain and the power that would come with it. He had a feeling he'd be seeing the agent. Baxter knew Phoenix's tenacity. He didn't reminisce on their battles, just the hell he put Phoenix through and the joy it brought him. At that moment Baxter Combs didn't think back but forward to the fruits of his labor. The money and rewards were great but the ripples he caused pleased him the most. He looked over to the case, now fuller, and for a brief moment pondered what could be found in the vials.

"We're coming up to the drop off point." The pilot said.

"Get ready, boys." Baxter told his crew and smiled a wicked grin.

Agents Phoenix and Martinie arrived at the Carbine City Credit Union. They got out and scanned the area, strangely desolate.

"Think he's been here?" Martinie asked.

"It's quiet. Too quiet."

Phoenix looked up suspiciously at the building's sign, which flickered.

"Let's go."

Phoenix drew his pistol and Martinie followed. They entered to find the staff, a few customers, and two security guards lying on the floor unconscious. Phoenix gave a curt nod to his partner. Martinie surveyed the lobby while Phoenix checked the bodies, their breathing and the familiar puncture wounds in the backs of their heads.

"Still alive." Phoenix said to his partner checking behind the counter.

He stood up and heard a faint clunking in the other room. The two looked at each other before Phoenix followed the sound. Martinie called their agency brethren to inform them of the location's situation. Agent Phoenix walked into the breakroom and heard it again, a thumping. His eyes peered over, scanning the room, when they landed on the closet. His pistol aimed with one hand, the other reached for the doorknob. He slung the door open to a startling scream. A young woman shivered and cried.

"NO! No, please no!" She whimpered and shielded herself the best she could.

"Okay. It's okay." He lowered his gun.

Martinie entered behind in a hurry. Phoenix turned and got him to lower his weapon.

"I just started! I don't want any trouble! I don't have anything!" She babbled and shook her head, slinging her curly hair.

"Don't worry, you're safe now. I'm Agent Phoenix. This is Agent Martinie." Both men holstered their firearms.

She wiped her tears away and tried to stop crying.

"Agents?"

They reassured her. Phoenix held his hand out and she took it.

They stood her up and dusted her off.

"Who...who were those guys?" She sniffled, wiping her face again.

"Bad news." Agent Martinie summed it up simply and returned to working the lobby.

"You're lucky to be alive, miss."

He led her back through the lobby, where she screamed upon seeing the bodies.

"Oh my God!" She cried out, flinching.

"They're okay. They're gonna be safe." Phoenix steadied her.

The people lying about gave her a fright. He walked her through, stepping over the unconscious bodies while Martinie spoke with the B team.

"They'll be here shortly." Martinie said hanging up.

"Good. We need to..." His phone went off with a sharp alert. "Phoenix."

"Agent Phoenix, Combs has been located. Carbon Bank & Trust. Our readings show that you're fourteen blocks away." They told him.

"On it. Phoenix out." He hung up and looked to his partner and the confused girl. "All right, wait for the others and get her in for an evaluation."

"You going after him?" His partner asked.

"You *know* I *am*."

Agent Phoenix exited and jumped in his cruiser.

"It's gonna be okay." Agent Martinie told her, hoping he was right.

She pulled her hair behind her ears and nodded, trying to not freak out.

Traffic was getting a little heavy for his usual road tactics so Phoenix turned his siren up to its maximum volume. The deep distortion and low bass shook the vehicles around his. Bystanders covered their ears. Holographic advertisements pixelated. Vendors' stands quaked in the agent's passing. Most importantly, everybody *moved*. Phoenix stepped on it. The siren's frequency rippled through the air, visible to those in the vicinity of the Agency craft. He swerved around the corners and maneuvered around cars that couldn't get out of the way, or were too slow to do so.

He tore through the city streets driven to finally get Baxter but also couldn't stop thinking about the people who were now vegetables at the hand of that maniac.

The pair of agents arrived at the Credit Union and Martinie led them through the scene. The bank's young new employee was taken in for a checkup. Help would soon be on its way to get the bodies to base so they can get the care they need until their minds can be returned to them.

The offices of the Agency were as busy as ever locking down Baxter's location, addressing incoming callers, and watching the light dot - representing the tracker in Phoenix's car - race around the board.

"Hell of a payday, boys." Combs said as he descended to the rooftop.

His crew followed and hauled the mechanism down the ladder. The pilot stayed, watched, and waited.

Meanwhile at home, dinner was cooking on the stove while Victor Louis-Phoenix continued to look up information on Colorado cabin stays, not knowing the danger his husband was currently pursuing. Agent Phoenix frequently feared the day his rogues' gallery would target Victor but would never express this worry aloud. Tobin warned him of his lifestyle and Victor knew the risks and proudly said "I do."

Right now, Phoenix couldn't think about that, only stopping the rogue of rogues. He could see the propellers of the helicopter as it settled into a landing, its inhabitants currently working their way through the Carbon Bank & Trust, a surprise to workers and any poor soul who decided to make transaction at that moment.

He sped up, screeched around the corner, narrowly missing the fire hydrant, and came to an abrupt halt. The agent ejected from the car and instantly heard the cries from inside. His pistol was pulled without a second thought. When he stepped to the door he could hear the struggle on the other side. His hand checked the door, quietly and slowly, to find it locked. Not surprised, he reared back and kicked the doors open. The Combs gang turned. Before they could react, Phoenix's eyes zeroed in on the machine on Baxter's arm and he fired at it. Sparks flew and its barrel dented closed.

The first teller lined up to end up in a vial exhaled with relief. Baxter's men opened fire on their interrupter. Agent Phoenix ducked back behind the door before peeking out and firing back. Combs tried his weapon but it had malfunctioned from the damage it had taken.

"Damn it." He grunted, retracting his arm.

The gunfight between Phoenix and the thugs gave the frightened civilians a brief moment to escape, but where to go? Baxter pulled a handgun from the holster in his coveralls and shot at the agent. The group of scared individuals crawled around to duck behind the counter.

The door and bookshelf Agent Phoenix had found himself behind wouldn't last long with the oncoming fire. He reached over and grabbed a pot holding one of the several decorative plants in the lobby and hurled it out to the open. Amidst the chaos, he popped out and shot the pot, blowing it into pieces, sending dirt and shards throughout. Baxter and company shielded themselves from the sharp cloud as Phoenix ran between them and dove over the counter. He landed with a thud, startling the shaken people hiding out. A barrage of shots hit the wall behind them and the counter itself was taking a beating. The customers and staff panicked.

"Don't worry. You're going to be fine. Just wait here." He told them. "I need you guys to stay strong."

Phoenix jumped up and fired several rounds over the counter.

"Give it up, Baxter!"

"Why does this sound familiar, Phoenix? I'd figured you'd retire after last time. I see you've recovered."

The agent pulled the wheeled chair over while the civilians were confused of this action. He threw it out and over as the Combs crew shot it to shreds before Phoenix popped up again blasting. After delivering round after round his pistol sparked and sputtered.

"Shit."

He ducked back down and ejected his clip, dead and powerless. He removed the other from its pouch. He checked to make sure it was still ready to go; it was lit up, fully charged. He reloaded when more shots rang out, but they sounded distant. The familiar close fire sounded in return. He leapt up to find the henchmen engaging in battle with Agent Martinie and the others coming to Phoenix's aid.

Three agents outside versus the three coverall-clad in a shootout while Martinie and the others tried to minimize collateral damage beyond the bank's perimeter. Phoenix joined the melee but

Baxter threw a plant in the way, bursting upon getting hit by the agent. Crouched behind the counter, the men and women tried not to scream at every shot fired. One of Baxter's men turned to fire back at Agent Phoenix while Combs grabbed his damaged goods and his valuable case and snuck out to the stairwell. One of Baxter's army fell, then another. Phoenix jumped the counter and clobbered the third with the butt of his gun to the back of his neck. Martinie and company rushed in.

"Baxter's getting away. Get these people out of here and get 'em checked out." With that, Agent Phoenix hurried to the stairwell.

Baxter Combs had gotten to the roof and was loading his gear when the door to the inside below was smashed open.

"This fucking guy..." Baxter muttered.

"Baxter!" Agent Phoenix yelled, before firing a nearby warning shot.

The man turned around.

"Give me the case, Combs. There are a million and one ways to make a buck, you don't have to do this."

"I know. I *want* to do this. Theft, murder, torment, these are just a few of my favorite things."

"You sick bastard."

Instead of taking the kill shot when he knew he wanted to, Phoenix holstered his weapon and went to rip him limb from limb. The two charged each other and met at the center of the roof, diving at one another with kicks and punches. Baxter's stocky stature was solid and he could take a hit with stride. Phoenix threw blows, his knuckles hitting the metal on his opponent's skin. Baxter struck back with body shots before delivering an uppercut to the agent's jaw. Phoenix swung his leg and kicked Combs in the head before spinning into him with an elbow. Baxter grabbed hold of Phoenix's waist from behind, pulled him up and back, and slammed him down to the rooftop. Phoenix swept Baxter's legs out from under him.

While the two threw rapid fire punches at each other, taking the pain as well as inflicting it, the pilot waited for his boss to dispose of the agent as he'd seen him do with so many before him. Agent Phoenix and Baxter Combs rolled in the brouhaha, one on top of the other, bluntly hammering down with tightly balled fists. Baxter pinned his foe down and wrapped his hands around his throat with a firm grip. Phoenix's hands shot up fast to Baxter's neck as well as the two choked each other to near unconsciousness.

Their hands gripped tighter until the agent managed to reposition his legs and flipped Combs over him. Both fought briefly for a deep inhale before getting up, finding they've fought to the edge of the roof.

"It's been fun, Phoenix, but it's time to blow." Baxter stepped over and sluggishly signaled the pilot to start the engine.

The propellers slowly started to spin when sparks flew from its center. Both Phoenix and his nemesis turned to find Agent Martinie shooting at the helicopter, stopping it before it fully started. Martinie rushed the pilot with his weapon poised ordering him out. Baxter faced Agent Phoenix in a rage.

"It's just never easy with you."

Combs pulled a knife from his boot and lunged at him, but Phoenix drew his pistol and shot multiple rounds into the roof beneath them. The shots blew a hole and, as he charged, Baxter fell in. He dropped the knife as his hands gripped the edge. He hung on when the hand that was around his throat prior grabbed his wrist, pulling him up. Phoenix straightened him upright and slugged him in the stomach, knocking the wind from him. His hands were pulled behind him and cuffed by Martinie. He looked over to see his pilot also cuffed, but appearing more scared of his punishment from Baxter than imprisonment. Other agents poured from the door. Combs stayed under Agent Martinie's aim as the agents approached. Phoenix wiped the blood from his lip.

"If we find ourselves here again, it won't end the same." Phoenix told him.

"No it won't, I promise you that, Agent Phoenix. We'll be seeing each other..."

The agents dragged the suspects away. The casing of vials, along with the weapon that extracted their contents, was taken from the chopper.

"Guess this storm came with a silver lining." Phoenix coughed.

"Yeah, we'll get everybody back to normal and he'll be put away in Bellview to rot. You okay?" Martinie asked.

"Heh, another day at the office." He spit blood.

Agent Martinie looked at his bruised and tattered partner and nodded.

"Let's get out of here."

Agent Phoenix entered the wing of the Agency dedicated to mental testing and examinations. He signed in and entered one of the many rooms, some currently occupied. He sat down in the close quarters holding his wounds. The door slid closed behind him.

"Phoenix. Tobin."

"Welcome Agent Phoenix." The soft voice said from the monitor before him. "Commensing test..."

An hour of questioning crossed between emotional and tactical to which he'd answer One, Two, or Three. His responses were, on average, a steady Two, but with the agitation of the evening's events he was answering more Ones. The closet-sized room monitored his brainwaves along with his heartrate. He tried to regulate his breathing and calm down from his fight with Baxter. Usually after a bout he was fine and level headed, thus the Twos, but Combs had a way of getting under his skin. The questions came at a rapid fire pace. If he didn't answer directly, the query was repeated. Practical and emphatic questions leap frogged one another as the numbered answers flew in return. The time spent helped mentally push aside his soreness. With the last question answered, he was released and made his way down the hall.

The room was quiet and he didn't speak to or acknowledge the other agents meditating cross-legged on the floor. The temperature was cool and the lights dim. He put in an ear piece and settled down in an open space, crossed his legs, and inhaled deeply. He focused hard, climbing his way through delightful scenes with Victor and knock-down-drag-outs with criminals, and soon, nothing. Blank canvas, a comforting solitude, and in time, the fight prior seemed a distant memory. Tobin floated weightlessly adrift while remaining stationary. There were no villains or urgent calls, nothing of grave importance. He was free. When the time elapsed, a soft beeping sounded from his ear piece and he found his way back to reality, refreshed.

NEW ARRIVAL

VICTOR STIRRED the sauce on the stove before checking its counterpart in the oven. Their stereo's surround sound was playing classic hip-hop as he bobbed his head and swayed his hips to the beat. With dinner reaching completion, he set the table and changed the music to some easy listening, good background dinner music. He dished out the pasta meal onto the plates and retrieved the bread from the oven, placing it in a basket to be set center table. Things were certainly calmer at home tonight than it was for Tobin Phoenix, putting his life on the line night after night.

After looking over the nice home cooked meal, Victor poured the glasses of wine. He'd hoped that Tobin would be home before dinner got cold. He wanted to turn on the news to see what his husband was surely dealing with but second thought it and kept the media off and the music on. He was about to sit down at the table when he took out his phone to take a picture of the meal. Seconds after posting it online, the door opened.

"Honey, I'm home."

Tobin's tone sounded sarcastic as he knew what his husband's reaction to his appearance would look like. He walked in as Victor left the dining room. His reaction was as expected. Victor's eyes widened and his mouth dropped seeing the post-fight Tobin. It wasn't out of the ordinary. The two smiled at one another.

"Rough day at work?" Victor asked with a smirk.

"Oh, you know, had to get a cat out of a tree."

"Let's get you out of these clothes." Victor sighed.

Tobin tried to help but was a bit sore for full motion. Victor unzipped the agent's jacket and took it off of him slowly, and then helped peel his shirt off. Tobin moaned and grunted in pain as it came off. The black shirt was tight enough on him without the sweat from the day's work. Victor ran his fingers over the deep bruises on his husband's body. Tobin tried to keep a tough exterior but winced at every touch.

"I need a shower and a drink."

"Well, sit down and have some dinner and then we'll get you in the shower."

Victor sat him down at the table and walked to the other side to join him.

"Nice." Tobin was impressed as he usually was when coming home to such a wonderful meal.

"Just a little something to take the tinge off." Victor winked.

"How was class today?" Tobin asked.

"Eh, sometimes I wonder if I'm getting through to any of these students. Some are remarkable and others don't seem to care, don't seem to even want to *try*."

"Babe," Tobin reached across the table and took hold of Victor's hand, "All you can do is your best and you do that on a daily basis. Even if they're not paying attention now, what you're saying will seep in. Trust me. The world needs more teachers like you."

"Well, thank you." Victor patted his hand. "I *am* trying. I keep telling myself 'if I can just help one student...' but then I know it's not enough and I want to help them all."

"I understand that all too well." Tobin chuckled.

"I think we both need a vacation." Victor eyed him over his glass.

Tobin smiled and held up his glass.

"No cats in a tree. No coming home looking like you were trampled in a stampede."

"And miss the look on your face?" Tobin joked.

"While I'm sure it's priceless, it's not a look I like donning. A week in some snowy mountains will do us both some good. No papers to grade, no villains to fight."

"And what if there's a yeti?"

"A yeti? *Really?*" Victor tore off a small bite of bread and threw it at Tobin. They laughed.

"This is excellent by the way." Tobin motioned to the food.

"Thank you."

They ate their meal in peace. No urgent phone calls. No fighting. Just good food and good company. The music in the background played its role. A night without the media streaming was much needed, especially after the night Agent Phoenix had had. When the meal was done, Tobin loaded the dishwasher. He turned to find Victor standing with a towel over his shoulder and a loofa in his hand and wearing a smile.

"New mission. Let's get you cleaned up, agent."

Victor joined Tobin in the shower. He inspected his agent husband's battle-wounded body while lathering him up. He instructed Tobin's arms up as he scrubbed him gently.

"Have you thought about when you're gonna retire?" Vic asked.

Tobin lowered his arms and any joy in his face dropped.

"C'mon, babe, I don't wanna talk about this right now."

"All right. Okay."

This conversation seldom came up but it usually ruffled Tobin's feathers.

"Look, I appreciate everything you do, just like Carbine City does, but I would like to have some time with my husband before he's whittled away."

"I understand. But the world's not safe enough for me to stop right now."

Tobin dolloped suds on Victor's head and kissed him. Victor rinsed off and left Tobin to finish up. When he was clean, Tobin came out to find two glasses of ice and a bottle of rum.

"Someone order a drink?" Victor asked.

Tobin sat in the bed and joined him in a drink. They turned on the TV and quickly changed from the news to some mindless television.

Meanwhile the armored van passed through the gates of Bellview. It came to a stop and parked as the agents got out and opened the back to remove Baxter Combs. With his hands and feet chained, they pulled him out of the back. He stopped momentarily with an agent to each side as they looked up at the towering institution.

"Home sweet home, Combs." One told him.

He didn't bother responding and they pulled him forward to the building. The three were met at the doors and led inside. The first wing, a grand hall with cells of various villains too much for the police department to handle, was alive with exclamations. Baxter was brought through like many before him. The hall fell silent as he passed. Eyebrows raised and the silence became murmuring.

Through the large doors, Baxter was brought into the next wing. He was taken to his cell where the guard swiped his keycard and the door slid open. A man – tall, muscular, and bearded – stood up from his bunk as Combs entered. Jethro Muldoon, rapist and murderer. Why he's in the likes of Bellview and not a normal prison with others of his crimes? Biomechanically enhanced genitalia, raping and killing simultaneously. With his twisted resume, he didn't understand the hoopla with Baxter.

Guards nervously kept their aim on Combs as others undid his shackles. They closed the cell and left as one guard stayed. He approached the new prisoner. Baxter leaned against the bars eagerly awaiting what was coming next.

"My cousin's still in care because of you. You took everything from him. His soul. Now he's just a vegetable. His family can't bring themselves to pull the plug because they still think there's a chance of getting him back." The guard told Combs, fighting back angry tears.

Baxter looked him in the eyes and a sly grin was tunneling to the surface.

"Well, they can keep waiting. I can't keep up with my supply but I'm sure he went for a pretty penny."

The guard grumbled and his jaw tightened and he was ready to leave before exacting excessive force.

"It depends on what he knew."

"And if he didn't know anything of importance? Just a regular guy like the others."

"Hmm, if there was nothing within him worth keeping, than they would've thrown out the vial. However, all sales are final." The grin was now thick.

The guard left to stew in his anger. Baxter chuckled and slapped the bars before turning around to see his new cellmate towering over him. Jethro looked Combs up and down, sizing him up. Jethro looked down at the new prisoner and snarled and turned to spit.

"So you're the big, bad Baxter Combs... Well, little man, in here," Jethro glanced around the cell with his arms out, "In *my house?* You're fresh meat."

He smiled and grabbed his crotch. Combs sized Muldoon up as well. Baxter hung his head for a moment and sighed, shaking his head.

"I guess...we all have to pay our dues."

His massive cellmate nodded and grinned with missing teeth. Baxter cracked his knuckles.

The guard turned the corner and entered a room where other guards were having a soda and a smoke.

"I know it ain't right, but I hope ol' Jethro has his way with Combs." He told the others who laughed.

Still angry, he walked over to pour a cup of coffee. The others continued their conversations before having to head back out. Everything came to a halt as Jethro's blood-curdling screams echoed through the halls and into the breakroom. Guards spit their drinks out and rushed out while the screams reached a fever pitch.

The newspaper card was thrown on the porch in its plastic casing. Victor opened the door, dressed for work, with his tie yet to be tied and picked it up before waving to the paperboy. He came back in, opened the case, and inserted the card into the media box beside the television. The headlines streamed as he returned to the kitchen. He poured hot coffee and freshly squeezed orange juice to go with the bacon, eggs, and toast he'd gotten up early to prepare.

Victor opened the bedroom door quietly and brought in the tray of food and drink where Tobin slept. Vic set the tray at the foot of the bed and walked around to Tobin's side.

"Breakfast in bed, sleepyhead." He said softly.

Victor softly laid his hand on Tobin's chest for a gentle wake, but he jolted up and grabbed his pistol off the nightstand, pointing it out with crazed eyes.

"WHOA! WHOA!" Victor jumped back with his hands up.

Tobin's finger was snug around the trigger, ready to squeeze, when he fully came to, to find his husband terrified with tears in his eyes. Tobin swallowed hard seeing the gun and Victor at the end of it. Shaken, Victor backed up.

"Vic..." Tobin said, trembling.

He dropped the gun and got up to hurry to Victor but he backed up scared.

"Baby, baby, I'm so sorry."

He pulled Victor in close but he wasn't in any mood to be held.

"What the hell, Tobin?" Vic shook with a lump in his throat.

"I know. I know. I'm sorry. I didn't mean to... I'm sorry."

Victor cried and tried to catch his breath from the shock. Tobin hugged him tightly, trying to ease him.

"I just wanted to make you breakfast in bed." Victor told him through tears and short breaths.

"I know, Vic. It won't happen again, I promise." Tobin put his hands on the sides of Vic's face. "I promise."

He kissed Victor and wiped his tears.

"No more bedside guns." Victor sniffled and shook his head.

"Agreed. No more bedside guns."

"I... I gotta get ready for work."

Victor left the room while Tobin cursed himself.

AN ACQUIRED TASTE

TRAFFIC OUTSIDE the Carbine City Diamond Emporium was its usual momentum. The sign hung above the entrance with a beautiful inlay and a holographic diamond. The flow in and out of the building wasn't nearly as thick it was on the sidewalk. Only those with the right amount of money would even dare enter. Window shoppers were discouraged and, without the funds proven, customers were shown to the door.

Inside was annoyingly civilized with sporadic customers being tended to and educated on why everything costs what it does. Among those various customers was one of the city's upper crust speaking with the Emporium staff.

"These are some of the finest diamonds on this side of the world, and *the* finest in Carbine City." The woman behind the counter said.

"They are gorgeous." The man said, running his fingertips along the double-plated glass.

"You did well coming in here and not one of these *jewelry stores*." She turned her nose up.

"Yes, I agree. Toy diamonds and plastic pearls compared to this," he eyed one stone in particular, "This is exquisite."

The woman smiled at the upcoming sale.

A large black van pulled up outside and stopped abruptly. No one paid it much attention until five women in large hazmat-like suits poured out. Their hair was up and they all wore goggles. It wasn't so much what they were wearing that caught the eyes of onlookers but what was strapped to them: luggage sized cylindrical tanks with thick hoses extending from them to the ladies' hands. They carried the hoses like machine guns and stormed the Diamond Emporium like soldiers going to war.

The first slung the door open and charged in. The others joined her in the same fashion and took their positions. Customers and staff alike turned to see them. Everyone froze. The air was still and quiet. A man looked up with his loupe in his eye. It fell out, breaking the uncomfortable silence, and his eyes had to refocus to see them. The group of women in suits and goggles with tanks on their backs aimed their hoses at everyone in attendance. The manager stepped out of her office, embarrassed.

"Um, excuse me, is it the *rats*," she whispered, "Do we have an infestation or something?"

The girls looked at her blankly then looked at each other and laughed.

"Yeah, we're here to clean house." One scoffed.

"Hands up! Diamonds out!" Another stepped further in.

The two security guards emerged, drawing their guns.

"Freeze! Drop your...weapons." The older guard stepped up.

His partner, younger by thirty years, stayed back with his pistol pointed.

The ladies giggled as the one in front reached back to flip the switch on her tank. It hummed loudly and the suction began. She directed the hose at the two men. The security in the back stood nervously but his gun never shook. The guard in front's gray mustache twitched.

"I said drop it!"

The older guard fired two rounds. The bullets were sucked into the hose. Their guns were pulled from their hands next, caught by the girls. She flipped another toggle, reversing the flow, and shot the bullets back at him. One in the shoulder, one in the arm, dropping him instantly. The young guard caught him on his way down.

"All right. Now that that's out of the way, let's go shopping."

Two of the ladies fired the newly acquired handguns at the thick casings, shattering the glass. Everybody screamed and ducked down. The team walked deeper into the Emporium and the vacuuming commenced. The scared citizens watched as diamonds flew overhead through the air. Stone after stone, big and small, sucked right up in the hoses. The tanks on their backs rattled with the whirlwind of jewels. The shards of glass that came with the merchandise were of no concern, they'd sort them out later. Their smiles grew wider the more they collected. The ladies noticed the jewelry on some of the customers, as well as the staff, and directed their devices towards them.

"That all looks like it cost a pretty penny. We'll take that, thank you."

Rings, bracelets, and necklaces came off of their persons right up the hoses. They tried to hold onto their belongings but let them go out of fear. A man took off his wedding band instantly without struggle and handed it over. His wife slapped his arm before hers was taken from her. The suction was strong; an older woman present held onto her wig. The five women broke off, getting every diamond seen. Bright shining stones moved with ease, glistening under the lights. The tanks were filling and the clatter within had lost its echo. The machines stopped sucking but the hum stayed.

"You." One of them addressed the cowering saleswoman. "Your selection out here is fine and all but I'd like to see what you have in the back."

"Get up." Another instructed, pointing the hose.

The woman got up from the floor, terrified. The manager stepped up.

"Excuse me, I'm the manager. She's not authorized. I'll do it."

"Okay." Their eyes questioned the woman. "Move it."

She hesitantly led two of the thieves to the back beyond the store floor. The saleswoman breathed a sigh of relief and sat back down.

"Everyone relax." The suited woman told everyone before addressing one of her cohorts. "Nobody leaves until we get everything."

The girl nodded and they continued taking in every diamond they could find, leaving no stone unturned. They walked behind the counters to get everything from underneath while still keeping an eye on everyone else. They reconvened in the center and kept everyone corralled while waiting for the girls in the back to finish up and return.

"What about anything else? Let's get their watches." One suggested.

"We got the time." They shrugged and went to work getting any and all accessories.

"Oooo, nice cufflinks." She commented before taking them off of a man.

The vault was opened in the back and the weaponized two lit up at the glorious sight. Millions upon millions of dollars' worth of assorted stones, predominantly diamond.

"We're gonna need another tank."

"You bet." She pulled her walkie, "We need one more in here."

"Jackpot." The receiver told the other two before retreating to the back to join the others.

The remaining two kept everyone under watch. The small crowd held hands and tried to stay strong.

"Be cool now." They told them.

Fearing for their lives, they complied.

"Freeze!"

The girls turned around to find three police officers entering with them in their aim. A commotion stirred amongst the people. A feeling of hope swelled within all of them.

"Give us the diamonds and put your hands up!" The leading officer commanded.

With the others currently busy, the two looked at each other with a giddy smirk.

"C'mon ladies, give it up."

The officers were nervous seeing the pair's attire. The girls slyly reached back to hit their toggles and aimed their hoses to the cops. The hum of the vacuum became a sharp whirring as diamonds, along with the broken glass, shot out with great velocity. The policemen were all riddled with the establishment's merchandise before they could get a shot off. The force pushed them back against the wall and they fell to the floor, dead.

People yelled from the floor fearing they'd be next.

"Well, they wanted the diamonds." One said to the other with a snicker.

Another flip of the switch and the bloody stones flew from the corpses into the hoses. They retracted every diamond, slinging blood droplets on the marble floors. The wet stones rattled and whirled in the tanks once more. The customers shivered, holding each other. One of the thieves noticed a shiny earring peeking out of the saleswoman's hair.

"Whoa, alright. We said everything. Earrings out, ladies."

Outside, most of Carbine City was none the wiser. A few

civilians stuck around to see what was going on but most went on about their day. The Agency cruiser pulled up behind the local squad cars.

"The boys in blue made it."

"Where are they? They should've brought out the perps by now... No, I don't like this. Let's go."

The earrings joined the jewels in the tanks as everyone handed them out.

The manager watched helplessly as the vault was drained of all of its contents. She thought about how she would explain this and if she made it out of the situation alive.

"That's almost the last of it." They said, sucking up every last shiny object.

The girls out front had sat the customers and staff together and watched them carefully.

"I don't suppose the word 'freeze' has any effect on you." Agent Phoenix said, giving the ladies a jump.

They spun around and tried their maneuver once more. Phoenix and Martinie had noticed the holes throughout the policemen and darted out of the line of fire, diving behind one of the side counters, avoiding the diamond spray.

"Okay. We got everything. Let's get out." The three returned.

"We got company."

The others posted up and the girls were in full force. Agent Phoenix paid attention to the diamonds being drawn back in and eyed the tanks strapped to their suits.

"We're done here, agents. We've got what we came for. You saw the cops. That doesn't have to happen to you."

Phoenix motioned to Martinie for cover.

"They say diamonds are a girl's best friend, but it looks like you've got enough friends." Phoenix told them and nodded to Martinie.

Agent Martinie jumped up from behind the counter and shot around them. In that moment Phoenix sprung up and shot the bottom of two of the tanks. Martinie dropped back down dodging the onslaught of diamond shrapnel, Phoenix followed. The tanks bottomed out and fell through, dropping piles of priceless jewels.

"Damn! Try to get this up!"

"We can't! There's no more room!"

Amidst their confoundment, they were caught off guard by the agents again as they fired at the remaining tanks. Diamonds fell as did all hopes for a successful heist. The tanks lightened on their backs and the suction in their hoses had given up. They still had the guards' pistols and shot at Phoenix and Martinie, barely missing them. But they were a bit overzealous with their gunfire and ran out of ammo; all the agents had to do was wait, and avoid getting hit. The women looked at each other in defeat. The smug smiles were gone.

They immediately tried to run but Phoenix and Martinie grabbed them by their tanks. One turned back and slugged Phoenix in the jaw. She tried to take another shot but he caught her fist, squeezing it, and spun her around. He went down the line cuffing all of them while Martinie kept his weapon on them.

"I don't know if I want to send you ladies to prison or to charm school." Agent Phoenix told them.

Martinie looked at the women and their bulky attire.

"I think you're gonna need a bigger car."

"Nah, this one's for the local boys. Call 'em up and get a van down here." Agent Phoenix said.

"Yes sir."

"Now, you ladies are gonna sit down right here and play the waiting game." His condescending tone came across perfectly clear.

They sat the group down on the floor and the customers and staff stood up. Everybody eyed the piles of diamonds in front of them.

"I don't think I should have to say it but nobody touches anything."

They nodded but were still entranced by the sight. They came in looking to buy a nice stone and here were mounds of them.

"Alvin?" Phoenix asked.

"Phoenix, hey." The agent and the young security guard shook hands.

He stood the older man up, his wounds bleeding out.

"Phoenix, we need to get him to a hospital."

"EMTs are on their way. Alvin, what happened here?"

They sat the bleeding gentleman down in a chair and both kept pressure on the wounds.

"Exactly what it looks like. Normal day, then they came suckin' up all the diamonds. Their tech looked like something one of *your* usuals would have but they don't really fit."

"You know the saying that seventy-five percent of businesses fail upon starting out? Same goes for heists."

The medics arrived as did more police officers.

"C'mon, Sam. Let's get you some help." Alvin stood his partner up to walk him to the ambulance.

"I'll catch you later, Phoenix." He told him in passing.

"Take it easy, Alvin. Hope he makes a full recovery."

"What in the hell?" The officers were shocked to find their brethren in blue shot to shreds.

While the bodies of the police were being examined, the girls were picked up and put in the back of the police van. The big black van was ransacked for evidence and impounded. The police checked out the people in the lobby for injuries and quotes.

"Some day." Martinie said.

"Yeah, and it's only..." Agent Phoenix looked at his watch. "Oh shit, I'm late. You take the car, it's not far from here."

"Sounds good."

Agent Phoenix ran faster than a jog, nothing that would raise a commotion. He bobbed and weaved around pedestrians and bumped into a couple along the way. The closer he was to the corner the more he picked up speed. He turned the corner and saw his destination in the distance. Phoenix sped up. He dodged people getting into cabs and citizens in hover-chairs. Finally, he arrived to the patio of Hartley's Pescatarian Diner to find Victor sitting, a tad annoyed. Phoenix approached.

"I am *so* sorry, Vic." Tobin sat down at the table, opposite Victor who was already shaking his head.

"I expected as much."

"You already order?" He asked.

"No, just a drink. Waiting to order once you got here."

"Can I get you something to drink?" The waiter asked.

"Uh, yeah, I'll take one of whatever he's having." Tobin answered.

"Alrighty. I'll take care of that for you."

The waiter left and Victor sipped his drink.

"What is that we're having anyway?" A curious Tobin asked.

"Ginger-Mint Soda." Victor smiled while Tobin winced. "They make it here."

"Ugh. Yay, can't wait."

"Whatever." They laughed.

A moment passed as Victor enjoyed his artisan soda while watching Tobin scan the menu as if it were evidence.

"So, you wanna talk about these dreams you've been having?" Victor asked.

"Say what?" Tobin glanced up from the menu.

"Your nightmares. They're more and more frequent and it seems like they're getting worse."

"I'm sorry, I don't really want to talk about it." Tobin said.

"You're overworked and stressed out. You need to get some rest."

"It'll be fine. Some warm milk before bed, some stretches, and I'll be good." He smiled hoping that would be the end of the topic.

"Mhm." Victor knew his husband's tactic and decided to drop the conversation.

"Here you are." The waiter returned with the agent's drink. "Are we ready to order?"

The couple looked at each other for a hot second with a nod.

"I'll have the shrimp salad." Victor answered.

"The salmon wrap."

"Alright. I'll get those orders right out to you." The waiter smiled and collected their menus before exiting.

"How's class today?" Tobin asked.

"I find myself having to change up strategies when I see them tuning out." Vic laughed.

"Just keep doing what you're doing. You'll reach them."

Tobin reluctantly took a drink and grimaced followed by a cough. Victor chuckled.

"I guess it's an acquired taste." He said, happily taking a drink himself.

Agent Martinie arrived at the Agency. Everyone was hard at work. A man with no arms was brought in by agents with his feet cuffed, behind them another agent carried two mechanical arms.

"Give you any trouble?" Martinie asked.

"No casualties but he put up a good fight."

"This is discrimination. I'm just a cripple. I've got no arms." The man said.

They moved on while the man behind them held up the machine limbs and shrugged. Martinie rolled his eyes and moved on to the hub where calls were being taken and security footage was examined.

"We have an arrest on Staple Street." A receiver stated. "Marla Manelli, aka *Screamer*."

"Agent." The workers greeted Martinie.

He nodded and looked everything over. He hadn't been with the Agency long and wanted to make sure he'd stay on it even when Phoenix wasn't around.

"Let's open city surveillance."

"Yes sir."

The room lit up with a collage of security footage from around Carbine City. Street corner after street corner, business after business, everywhere the Agency had eyes was illuminated before them.

"Okay, let's see what we got."

They eyed the footage for anyone or anything in need of their assistance. While they searched, Martinie noticed the woman known as Screamer was brought in with a cybernetic muzzle on.

"Never a dull moment." He said as they took her away to process her.

He returned his attention to the city in need. Commuters made their way across town in vehicles and on foot. Gardens were watered and dogs were walked. Nothing seemed out of the ordinary at the moment, but...

"Wait, what's that? Sector two, fourth quadrant."

They maximized view on the location but what Martinie saw he couldn't describe.

"Here you are." The waiter delivered the couple's food to their table.

"Looks great." Victor smiled.

"Thank you." Tobin said looking at his salmon wrap.

"If you need anything else, just holler." The waiter exited.

"Any more thoughts on our vacation?" Victor asked digging into his shrimp salad.

"I'm still torn." Tobin took a bite. "Mmm damn that's good."

"Tobin, I'm serious. You need a break. You're already not sleeping well. You keep going and you're gonna burn out."

"I'll be fine. Trust me. I'll take a break and rejuvenate. Look, I'm on a break right now." He smiled holding up his food.

"Yeah, yeah."

A guttural roar cracked through the sky like thunder and elongated before tapering off with a siren-like wail. Tobin and Victor looked over as did the other diners out on the patio. People ran down the street screaming as the roaring continued. A terrible animalistic bellowing that brought fear to anyone that heard it.

"Sorry babe," Tobin shrugged. "I gotta go."

Agent Phoenix wiped his mouth off and rushed off to where everyone was running from.

"Check please!" Victor yelled for the waiter. He looked at their plates and shook his head. "Some break."

Dust clouded Agent Phoenix's office as he, Martinie, and others entered. The men walked in, brushing off dust and debris, their uniforms torn and slightly bloodied. They sat, bruised and battered and groaning from exhaustion.

"What the hell *was* that thing?" One of the agents asked.

"I don't know. Some sabretooth-crocodile-mutant cat thing." Martinie answered.

"The fangs on that beast."

"And the claws, good grief."

"How did the *crazy cat lady* keep that thing concealed for so long?" Phoenix asked rubbing his arm.

"You alright?"

"Yeah. Thing had some reach on it." Phoenix nodded.

Agent Brick popped his head in.

"Guys, get a load of this: the old lady has a ball of yarn the size of a train car in her backyard." He told them.

"Great. Imagine the cost of keeping that thing fed."

"One other thing, Agent Phoenix. Everyone's consciousness is restored." Brick informed him.

"Good. And Baxter's locked up." Phoenix nodded. "Good work, Brick."

"Just one more thing. We lost one during the transfer. Went into cardiac arrest."

"Damn. I hate to hear that. Alert their family."

"Already on it." Brick left.

"We lose 'em even when we save 'em." Agent Martinie said, looking at Agent Phoenix deep in thought. "But at least Baxter's behind bars and that beast today is gone. It could've killed a lot of people and we stopped it." He tried to cheer his partner up.

"Hey, I think it liked you, Martinie. Its tail wagged when it picked you up." One of the men coughed. They laughed.

"Yeah and that damn tail leveled a department store." Phoenix said.

The laughter died down quickly.

"Well, you put it down, Phoenix."

"It took long enough. Now the streets smell like burnt hair."

"Well, nobody died and the old bag's in custody so everything worked out."

"We're worked out all right." Martinie said holding his leg.

Agent Phoenix stood up, holding his ribs.

"I'm going to the medic to make sure everything's where it's supposed to be."

The others seconded that and left the office with limps and grunts.

Beyond an enlarged, scaly and monstrous feline and a botched diamond job, Carbine City was still living and breathing. The city was prone to bugs and viruses but it always found them and cleaned it up. It pulsated electric and radiated a certain drive in its inhabitants. Everyone that was able to worked, to some capacity. Jobs were assigned according to skill sets. 'When everyone's talents come together, Carbine City stands tall!' As one famous headline read.

The air was crisp and clean as the vehicles ran off of the steam of distilled water. A man had just pulled up to a fuel station and got out to punch in his code. While fueling, he looked out at the four-way intersection to his right and he squinted to better see what he thought he saw. Humongous bush-like bundles of cat hair blowing across the street like a tumbleweed. They were a long ways away from the dark days of the great drought roughly nine years before when fuel was depleted. For a while the bike lanes were more occupied than standard driving lanes. When the drought was over, dealerships were raking it in. The incessant advertising led people to buy new vehicles instead of dusting off long-sitting cars waiting for fuel.

News vendors slid their SD cards into cubes that displayed the holographic headlines about a foot above it. Potential customers scrolled through the headlines and mused over the celebrity gossip. Produce vendors sold by the seed in partnership with their neighbors selling germination spheres.

Local Carbine City police stopped muggers and investigated break-ins. Despite the equality the city represented, some citizens wanted more and petty crime was common, but it never seemed to amount to much in the end. The criminals who'd either had enough of being small time crooks or had severe vendettas took it a step further and that's when the Agency got involved.

A young man slowly passed the newsstand and looked around. He *snatched* an armful of cards and took off.

"Hey! HEY! Stop him! Police! Police!" The vendor shouted.

A cop was flagged down and they raced to find the thief. Leaving a trail of cards behind him didn't help and the police apprehended the man. Another day on the beat for Carbine City cops.

Agency technicians came out for the monthly maintenance on surveillance cameras. The eyes on the city were polished, tightened, and recalibrated. On occasion their work was watched by curious civilians.

"Nothing to see here." They'd tell them before shooing them off and returning to work.

THE MAILMAN COMETH

MEANWHILE ACROSS town, the mail had been delivered. The truck had come and gone. The light on top of the mailbox blinked green. Mr. Wright came from his home, not too long after getting dressed, to retrieve it. He punched in his postal code and opened the box. Upon briefly sifting through the stack, he saw his normal mail comprised of bills and ads. Something new stuck out, however, as he found an envelope labeled Final Notice. Usually mail like this came with an obvious air of junk or scam, such as the You've Just Won letters that came weekly, but this envelope didn't carry any of those attributes. It looked quite official with a certain grim quality about it. Mr. Wright eyed it suspiciously before looking around his neighborhood, seeing nothing out of the ordinary.

His neighbor across the street was washing his car while the neighbor to his left was watering her garden. When she was finished, she pointed a remote control at it, pressing a button. Light flickered atop the flowers before being stimulated by the electricity and stood up straight, blooming. Mr. Wright turned and walked back up the walkway to his home. One more quick shuffle through the mail and he put the bulk of it on the counter, save for the ominous envelope. Addressed to him with his personal identification number printed for the world to see, Final Notice was stated in bold red letters.

"What *is* this?" He asked aloud.

He lifted the tab on the back to an audible click but, before he could remove its contents, abrupt tragedy had already taken place. His neighbor had just dried his car when the house across the street erupted into a great explosion. The home shattered, throwing its pieces and flames around the perimeter and into the sky. Neighbors came outside to see the cause of the noise and commotion and saw the damage. Mr. Wright was obliterated along with his home. The Final Notice wafted in the air unscathed by the flames.

On another block across town, the slot in the door opened and the mail was fed through, being taken in by the mouth of a dog. The golden retriever trotted through the house to his masters.

"Good boy." The woman said, taking the mail and patting his head. "Let's see what we have... Final Notice? For what?"

She set the rest of her mail down next to her coffee as she inspected the envelope. After reading her name and identification number, she lifted the tab...

"Alright. Get your rest and stay hydrated." Agent Phoenix said, before hanging up the phone.

Agent Brick entered the office with urgency.

"We got four bombings this morning. Residential areas."

"Any leads?"

Agent Brick laid out four clear bags, each containing a Final Notice envelope with the insides and the rims of their openings blackened.

"These were found at each location."

Agent Phoenix eyed them.

"Okay. Run a test on these and see what makes them so inflammable."

"Already on it."

"Wait..."

Agent Phoenix opened his top drawer and removed a pair of gloves, snapping them on. He opened one of the bags and slid the envelope out, inspecting it. Inside was black and the sides were stretched slightly. His brows furrowed as Brick watched Phoenix think to himself. While he wanted to ask what him was thinking, he knew better than to interrupt the process. Agent Phoenix quickly reached for the next, and the next, finding the same thing across the board. Blackened, stretched material comprising an ordinary envelope. His mind raced and his eyes darted.

"This was it? This is what survived?"

"Yes sir."

"Take these to the lab and find what they're made of." Agent Phoenix stood up. "I gotta find that mailman."

"Sir?"

"The explosions came from these. And find out any connection between everyone who received one."

Agent Brick looked around.

"And Agent Martinie?"

"He's home sick today. Caught a nasty bug from some bad takeout." He said, taking his clips off of their chargers before sliding one into his pistol.

Agent Brick left. Before leaving the office himself, Tobin snatched up the phone and dialed.

"Hello?"

"Victor, don't open the mail."

"Okay... What's going on?"

"Babe, just listen to me and don't open the mail. Okay?"

"Alright. Okay."

"I gotta go. I love you, I'll tell you later."

"Love you too. Be safe."

Agent Phoenix hung up the phone, strapped on his holster, and left.

Agent Phoenix's cruiser flew down the street, its sleek aerodynamic body weaving around drivers on the road effortlessly. Wind barely pushed against the other vehicles but the laser-like speed and the deep distorted booming siren of the agent's car caught the attention of those behind the wheel. Some instinctively froze, momentarily believing they were a person of interest until the agent on the hunt was well beyond them.

"No, don't call the post office about this!" Agent Phoenix told his colleague via radio. "We don't have time for the Postal Inspectors to investigate, and we also don't need to give the bomber any heads up. Hold on!"

Just ahead an alleyway erupted, throwing flames and debris out into the street. Vehicles swerved and crashed into one another. Agent Phoenix dodged miniature pileups before coming to a hissing halt.

"Martinie, you sure picked a hell of a time to order dumplings."

The agent got out and immediately checked his surroundings.

Smoke and dust was still thick and falling. Civilians tended to others hurt and shook up.

"You guys alright?" He asked.

A man promptly nodded while rubbing his neck.

"I need you to check some of the others; can you do that for me?"

Agent Phoenix's request was direct and invoked a certain confidence in the man. He finished rubbing his slightly-whiplashed neck looking into the agent's eyes. He nodded again.

"Y-yes. Yes I can."

He got out of his car as Agent Phoenix continued on to the next. Both men quickly checked the surrounding drivers and their passengers, recruiting more to help. Their party grew and assisted those in need.

"You okay?" The agent asked a coughing pedestrian.

Her eyes were watery, stinging, and her face was filthy from the thick cloud. She coughed and hacked as Agent Phoenix patted her back and directed her to one of his momentarily deputized citizens as they shuffled her away to get water. A child's crying caught his ear. He looked around but the airspace was still chaotic and he couldn't quite detect where it was coming from. Men and women helped pry one another from pinned vehicles and aided them in limping to safety. The smoke cleared, however briefly, as the crying child was finally spotted. The agent's heart dropped for a second seeing the kid in distress and he made his way to them, fanning the dust along the way.

"They won't wake up!" The child screamed before babbling.

Agent Phoenix looked at the parents in the front seat, unconscious and bleeding. He checked their pulse and leaned their heads back as their breathing became more apparent.

"You're not gonna be an orphan today, kid." He said, gently pulling the child from the broken window. "Need some help over here!"

"I can help." A woman approached and the child was exchanged.

She seemed as rattled as everyone else but was determined. Agent Phoenix turned his attention once more to the parents. The X-patterned seatbelts were jammed. He pulled the knife from his boot and cut the straps as the bodies slumped forward. Others came to aid the agent in retrieving them when a slight hiss, once unnoticeable, became louder. Phoenix stopped and listened carefully while a few helpful civilians pulled the parents out as gently as possible. The agent leaned in closer to where the leaky sound was coming from. His eyes widened.

"It's gonna combust! Everybody get back!"

Agent Phoenix hoisted the child's father, significantly heavier than his wife, over his shoulder. With a quick look and hand movement from the agent, two others put themselves under each arm of the woman.

"Back! Everyone back!"

The unconscious parents were pulled to safety and the area cleared quickly.

Just as he suspected, the car popped and hissed louder before exploding. Everyone in the vicinity ducked back and shielded themselves from the now-scrap pieces flying about. A quick check and everyone was safe - as safe as one could be in such a situation. No fatalities in the street and minimal injuries. Agent Phoenix eyed the still-smoking alleyway before stepping in. The walls on either side were thick with blackness from the explosion and the resulting smoke. A dark alley on a bright day. He inspected the shadow painted area to find, along with the scorched trash, scraps of clothing - bloodied and burnt. The sound of assistance arriving was behind him. EMTs and backup from the agency got out of their respective vehicles to assess the crowd and its damage.

Agent Phoenix walked in further. Obliterated bits of what used to be body parts were strewn about the long alley. If it wasn't for the compact explosion it would've been a bloody mess; however, as it stood, every bit of flesh was eviscerated. He kneeled down to get a closer look, counting more than a couple of ribcages. Amidst the ashes was a familiar envelope. Final Notice - complete with a name and identification number. The inside of it identical to the envelopes brought in to him prior.

"Now, who opens their mail in an alleyway?" He asked himself.

"Agent Phoenix." Agent Brick said upon entering the alley.

Phoenix turned and held up the envelope before standing up. Brick looked at their surroundings and shrugged.

"Here?"

"Same thing I wondered. Get the lab boys on this alley. We got multiple bodies. And find what you can about the recipient." He handed the envelope over.

"Yes sir." Agent Brick placed it in a small evidence bag.

"Everyone out there clear?"

"Yes sir. Minor injuries. More shook up than anything. Roadway's clear."

"Good. I got to stop this bastard."

He walked past Brick to his car in the street. The agent took a look around the area and its damage and shook his head. The bones on the ground smoked and pieces of the brick walls crumbled and fell below.

Victor sat at home watching news of bombings and worried for his husband. He opted to not even go out to the mailbox despite its blinking green light.

"Tobin, please be careful..." He exhaled.

It hadn't taken Victor long after Tobin's call to phone his sister to give her the same warning he had received. She questioned but even he didn't have an answer, just a word of caution.

Less cautious at the moment was Agent Phoenix, speeding down the road with fluidity. His eyes shifted to either side, seeing the green inbox lights in passing. With one hand on the wheel, the other flipped radio.

"Phoenix to base."

"Come in, Agent."

"We need units out to check all incoming mail."

"Sir?"

"Check the mail. Confiscate it all if necessary. Nothing is opened or released without authorization."

"Sir, that would take-"

"Phoenix out."

Radio off, the agent accelerated onward.

"Where are you, you son of a bitch?"

No further explosions were detected along his trek. Even with the speed, his eyes kept the green lights in his peripheral. The red lights symbolizing an empty box were few and far between.

The blinking green was aplenty and he knew that it would be a headache to get them checked, but it needed to be done. He switched on the radio for an outgoing call once again.

"Agent Tobin Phoenix requesting postmaster contact."

"Processing..."

"This is Postmaster Carter. How can I assist you, Agent Phoenix?" The postmaster's voice came through fractured and skipping as the signal cut in and out.

"I need the tracking coordinates for all of your available mail trucks."

"No can do. Our system's been down all morning. We barely have communications out. Everything inside is cold. No tracking, and can't receive word from carriers." The static and dipping signal continued.

"Then I need your carrier registry."

"Agent Phoenix, you're breaking up. I can barely..."

The radio blipped and bleeped upon losing signal.

"Shit!" He slammed his fists onto the wheel.

The world flew by him at tremendous speeds on his hunt. While he searched for the mail truck, he thought about whether or not the carrier in question had taken a new vehicle or was on foot. Random drivers dodged the agent's cruiser while excited at the notion of witnessing a high speed chase. A race against time. A race against the bomb. His hands gripped the wheel tighter. With his eyes dead-set on the road ahead, the surrounding visuals seeped in through his peripheral, instantly being catalogued, not only if they were a threat or not but the level of danger they would carry. Among these flashing images was a big mailbox on a corner, a relay box.

A thought that hadn't occurred to him arose: *Is all this chaos from the carrier, or are they actually just mailed? Could I have the wrong man in my sights, unknowingly delivering deadly material?*

Then he saw it - an opening between cars parked on the curb. A hard jerk of the wheel and passersby watched as his cruiser spun into the spot perfectly, coming to a stop.

"Wow." One boy said to another.

Agent Phoenix got out of the vehicle and hurried to the box. He knew it was a gamble on whether anything was in the box or not. As he expected, the box wasn't an easy open. He pulled his pistol and shot the latch. Bystanders jumped in shock. He turned back to onlookers.

"Official business. Nothing to see. Go on about your day."

The agent opened the relay box to find a pile of mail. He crouched down and rifled through it in search of those bold red letters. Junk mail, ads, coupons, bills, and more bills. No Final Notice found, not even in the normal capacity. He looked around and saw the green inbox lights blinking at the small businesses around him.

'They got their mail but the pickup here wasn't made.' He thought.

He pulled his phone out while still waving onlookers off. The call was ended before it rang as something came into focus. A woman across the street, half a block down, was retrieving her mail. The agent put his phone away, replaced the stack of mail, and closed the box the best he could.

The woman closed her mailbox and briefly thumbed through her small assortment. Phoenix ran over to catch her before she went inside.

"Excuse me, ma'am."

She turned, guarded.

"Agent Phoenix," he flashed his ID quickly before continuing, "I have a couple of questions, but first I'm going to have to check your mail."

She held up her mail with a slight scoff.

"It's just mail."

"Ma'am..." He held his hand out.

She begrudgingly handed it over. It didn't take him long to sort through it. Mail much like he'd seen in the relay box.

"Okay, you're good." He said returning her mail to her.

"Huh?"

"Do you know about what time your mail usually arrives? Do you have the same mailman every day? Happen to know their name? Could you identify them?" His eyes never wandered from hers in his direct questioning.

She stood, stunned by the barrage of questions.

"I work nights most of the time so I'm asleep when he comes. So... I have no idea. Am I in some kind of trouble?" She nervously asked.

"Oh, no ma'am. Just thought you could help."

"I don't know anything. Sorry."

"That's all right. Thank you for your time."

She returned to her home while Agent Phoenix made his way back to his cruiser. He wasn't hurrying and kept his eyes out for anything suspicious, or at least a clue that could help point him in the right direction. He thought of the route records but knew it would take too long to get a hold of the postmaster again followed by tracking down recorded routes. Too long in the current circumstances - death delivered to one's door. He stopped and scanned his surroundings.

"The known explosions were from that end of town." He said, pointing in that direction before motioning back over his shoulder. "And some of these people are just now checking their mail..." He turned back again to see more green blinking lights on the block.

His thought concluded with action as he raced to his vehicle. The car parked in front of him had left. He jumped in and sped off. His eyes darted all over the landscape trying to lock on to a potential target. His phone rang. A quick glance and he saw the picture of Victor and him in front of a beautiful stone fountain with his husband's name blinking.

"Fuck, babe, not now."

He weaved around more cars at a climbing speed. Tobin quickly realized that something may be wrong and answered.

"Everything okay?" No time for a formal greeting.

"I'm fine. I'm worried about you. There was another bombing."

"Another one!? Vic, I gotta go."

"Be safe."

"Always."

He hung up and flipped the radio.

"Dispatch."

"This is Phoenix. Get me Brick."

"Yes sir."

If it wasn't for the official vehicle with its siren radiating, other drivers would assume someone was out for a drunk and reckless joyride. A drunken speedster with impeccable proficiency behind the wheel. Some drivers moved out of his way, not wanting to be stopped for obstructing justice. But Phoenix was too fast for most and sped around them. His tires spun so fast they were practically airborne and the engine's steam trail snaked around the traffic like sporadic piping.

"Brick here."

"You wanna tell me why I had to hear from my *husband* about the new bombing?" His temper rose before the question was finished.

"Sir, it *just* happened."

Agent Phoenix rolled his eyes and grit his teeth.

"Information."

"We're working on it. It's a real shitstorm."

"Keep working. Call the local news station and order a temporary cease open on all mail."

"On it."

"Phoenix out."

He emerged over the peak of a hill and in a split second his sight sharpened. Everything became a sea of stark black and white contrasted only by the rows of tiny red lights on either side. The first turn up ahead to the right illuminated and he had to act on his sudden hunch. Agent Phoenix slowed momentarily as the truck to his right moved ahead. The cruiser turned and darted into the next lane and spun around the corner. Green lights were visible as he made his way down the street, but not for long. A few blocks down, the green blinking lights gave way to solid red. And at the end of the serviced homes was a billowing of smoke and steam. The agent's vehicle slowed and approached it. The mail truck he'd been on the hunt for, crashed into a post, totaled.

Agent Phoenix stepped out and drew his weapon before moving on his target with caution. Inspecting the accident he noticed the wreck was fresh. His gun elevated and he peeped the scene. The vehicle was devoid of life. He checked his surroundings. No one around, save for onlookers peeking out of their windows. They quickly backed behind the curtains once he'd seen them. The hatch to the back of the truck dangled open. Agent Phoenix kicked it open fully and forced his pistol inside. A man lay in his shorts with a look of terror stretched across his face and two bloody bullet holes in his chest. His uniform and mail bag were nowhere around.

"That answers one question I had..."

"Phoenix come in. Come in, Agent Phoenix."

He holstered the pistol but stayed alert and made his way back to the car.

"Phoenix. What do you got?"

"The bodies in the alley. All younger than the targeted recipient of the letter. Reports had been abound of mail theft in the neighborhood. Apparently they finally stole the wrong envelope."

"Well, we got a body here. Presumably the real mailman, shot and stripped."

"I'll call assistance."

"Good. Any word on the connection between them yet?"

"Thank you." He said to someone else at the station. "Just got it in. They all used to work for the law office of Sims & Simms. The last name on the list is Cheryl Barton, currently residing at 920 September Street."

"Any leads on the suspect?"

"Nothing yet. It would appear they made their fair share of enemies."

"Alright. Phoenix out." He switched off the radio before turning on his location scouter. "Location."

"Burr Avenue." The car's computer system stated.

"Burr Avenue to September Street."

"Three blocks west."

He floored it but kept his siren off and turned onto Chestnut Street. Looking back and forth, side to side, he didn't see anything out of the ordinary, and moved on. The next was Samson. Another dead block, but he knew he was getting closer. Wait. He spotted someone. The agent was about to pursue when the man was heard calling for his dog, who eventually trotted back to him. On the opposite side of the street, an elderly man was checking his mail. The order he'd had sent for the news crew must not had been aired yet. Justice never worked as fast as he'd liked. Onto September Street now.

An average neighborhood street, one he knew would soon be a place of terrible tragedy if he didn't work fast. His gaze scanned the area quickly before he spotted him. The mailman trotted down the street in his uniform blues with his bag over his shoulder, whistling all the while. Agent Phoenix assessed the perp - older, grizzled, and thin with a scraggly beard. His foot slammed down and he sped forward towards the gleefully oblivious suspect. Hearing the oncoming vehicle, the man stopped and turned. The agent's cruiser spun around the mailman, stopping inches from him. The man threw his arms up, stunned, delivering a gasp and false starts.

"Hands up! Drop the bag!" Agent Phoenix commanded exiting the vehicle with his pistol poised.

"Uh, uh, hey man. I'm just walkin'." He shook and shivered where he stood.

"Drop the bag!" He repeated.

The man dropped the bag and his hands shot back up.

"Hands behind your back."

The agent approached the man cautiously, keeping his weapon on him with one hand and reaching for his cuffs with the other. He turned the man around and placed the rod to his wrists. His thumb pressed the center square and the rod curled and closed tightly. The man murmured and grunted indistinctly while his arrester kneeled down to check the bag. He unzipped it furiously and carefully rifled through its contents.

"I can't believe this. Guy can't even walk around anymore without the law harassin' ya." The man grumbled.

"Just walkin' around, huh? Make any special deliveries on your walk?"

Amidst his questioning, what the agent found was an

assortment of various mail but no sign of the dreaded envelope.

"Deliveries?" The man chuckled. "I ain't the *mailman*."

"Oh yeah?" Agent Phoenix stood up.

"Fella switched me clothes and gave me fifty dollars. I wasn't about to pass that up. Them smelly ol' rags ain't been washed in a minute." He laughed once more.

The agent's eyes grew wide.

"Which way did he...?"

Before he could finish his question, he spotted someone upon his scanning that would match his temporary suspect's outfit description. Phoenix quickly uncuffed the man and took off on foot.

"Hey, what about me!?" The scruffy man asked, rubbing his wrists. "Oh well..."

He looked down at his uniform and smiled. He adjusted his hat, picked up the bag, and left, whistling once again.

Agent Phoenix was getting closer and he could see the real target heading for the house at the end of the street. Younger than the man prior, clean shaven, and wearing old ratty clothes littered with holes and tears. The only thing of his image that stuck out was the official post office badge, allowing him access into the boxes. He wasn't filling mailboxes on his way, his ruse was done and had one target left. The agent picked up speed but the drop-off was completed. The man slid the envelope in and shut the box with a prideful grin across his face. While every mailbox around them held a steady red light, this address's box blinked green.

He turned and walked away casually, exhaling. His smile wouldn't last, he knew that, but he was satisfied with what he'd accomplished. The bomber wouldn't get far before he was speared from behind to the ground. Agent Phoenix tried to cuff him when he was down but he squirmed and fought back. He turned and elbowed the agent in the face before spinning around to punch him with his other hand. Phoenix returned the punch and soon the two were rolling around in a flurry of blows; punching, kicking, knees and elbows.

A woman exited her home dressed and ready for work. Cheryl Barton walked down to her mailbox with her briefcase in hand when she saw the two men. They saw her as well.

"Don't open that mail!" Agent Phoenix yelled.

He tried to get to his feet but was kicked in the ribs by the assailant. She stepped back from the mailbox stunned. Miss Barton squinted, focusing closer on the two.

"Lannerman? William Lannerman?" She asked, surprised.

The man, now identified, threw a right cross but the agent caught his fist and delivered an uppercut. His jaw cracked and he crumbled before taking another punch to the forehead. Agent Phoenix had gotten his man. He cuffed him before addressing the woman.

"Do you know this man?"

She nodded, giving the suspect a dirty look.

"His name's William Lannerman."

"You all sentenced my father to prison and he died in there! He died, and it ruined my mother!" Lannerman shouted through a bloodied jaw, angrily and painfully.

"His father was a weapons dealer. Most of it stolen, military grade." She explained.

The man writhed in pain on the ground while Phoenix stretched and tended to his own wounds. Lannerman cried for his parents, as well as the pain of an ass kicking.

"Ma'am, I'm going to have to take your mail."

"What did he put in there?"

"Nothing you wanna open..."

The current of the office had become less turbulent after the capture of Lannerman, or *The Mailman*. The calls came in the same but most didn't require the use of the agents. While the Mailman had made a splash in such a short period of time, he still didn't make the lit-up list upon the wall as it was mainly comprised of repeat offenders. The coffee kept coming as often as the calls did. Workers watched holographic surveillance footage while assessing the crime scene from their seats, whether that be a domestic dispute or a robbery.

Agent Phoenix sat in his office with Agent Brick across from him; both enjoying the moment of peace.

"So the guy kept crying about his mother and father?" Brick asked.

"Yeah, even as I took him in. He cried out about his mother more than his father. I guess her husband's arrest and death messed her up pretty bad." Phoenix theorized.

"So, a mama's boy with bombs..." Brick thought aloud.

"Ugh, I hate mama's boys."

"How the hell did he do it anyway?"

Agent Phoenix removed from his desk a plastic bag containing what looked to be a flashcard-size computer chip.

"Best way I can describe it is compact plastique."

He pointed to a small segment as Brick leaned forward for a closer look.

"This here's the trigger point. This," Agent Phoenix set down the envelope beside the explosive card, "Is the detonator."

He motioned to Agent Brick to lean in. He obliged, leaning forward as Agent Phoenix held the envelope up to the light.

"See it?" He asked.

Under the light, a strange pattern became visible; angular, measured.

"Man..." Brick shook his head. "So, why deliver the other mail?"

Both men returned to their original positions. The world beyond the office, a whirlwind of information at different volumes.

"His plan. Had to play the part."

"Huh... You think killing the real mailman was a part of the plan, or was it unexpected?"

Agent Phoenix paused for a brief moment while searching his mind.

"The blood..."

Agent Brick looked back at him questionably.

"The bum's uniform had no blood on it. No holes. The mailman, the *real* mailman, was shot in the chest. He would've had to have made him strip first." Phoenix explained.

"Well, he was determined."

"He was but it doesn't sound like he had much of an exit strategy."

Brick nodded, agreeing. The phone rang and Agent Phoenix promptly answered.

"Phoenix."

He pulled his head away from the phone upon hearing violent hurls of vomit.

"It's Martinie." Phoenix told Brick.

"I'll let you deal with all that." Brick stifled his chuckle and left the office.

"Sorry, boss, still getting this damn bug out of my system." Martinie coughed hard. "I saw you got the bomber. One sec..."

Phoenix pulled away again as Martinie continued getting sick.

"Agent, go back to bed and drink lots of water. Flush out your system. I've got..." Agent Phoenix looked at a fairly empty desk and shrugged. "Paperwork to get to."

"Alright. I think that's a good ide-uh...uhh..."

The sickness flowed as Agent Phoenix rolled his eyes, matching the look of disgust on his face. The conversation ended as Phoenix hung up and exhaled. Martinie hung up and threw his phone to the side on his way to the trashcan.

Agent Phoenix looked out of the glass wall to see the worker bees busy buzzing about. The office was lit by incoming hologram calls backed by switches and lights of the control center. Various tongues, native to the distressed callers, were spoken for more accurate assistance. Issues were assessed and sorted through to determine what would be in need of the agency and what would be best left to local cops. Maintenance tightened up the power base for the agents' pistol clips. The custodian used plenty of disinfectant and cleaned the large wall screen as well as the holo-lenses at each station intermittently. Weekly reports came in on the holdings of Bellview. Reports and messages not needed beyond a single read were not shredded, but incinerated for security purposes. Fuel was refreshed and the receivers stayed sharp, staying objective to each call. New information was locked in. Suspects were logged into the database and victims or their families were checked up on after ninety days of the incident requiring an agent's presence. Justice was being served at its most calculated.

Agent Phoenix watched the hive with pride before receiving a new call. It was time to get back to work.

A TRIP TO BELLVIEW

WILLIAM LANNERMAN, The Mailman, was delivered to Bellview. Wrists and ankles chained, he walked in short steps as he was led through the doors. The long halls were lined with reinforced cells containing a who's who of violent, cunning criminals detained by the Carbine City Agency. The walk was long and Lannerman felt he certainly didn't belong with the likes of the others. To his right, behind thick bars, was a woman known to the general public as *The Pianista*. A piano teacher who snapped and began to advertise free lessons...only to strangle her students with piano wire.

Up to his left, as they continued walking, stood a large man. His hands gripped the bars and he growled and began to grow. Lannerman watched from his peripheral in shock as the man's large fists dwarfed the bars, now appearing the size of wires. Dubbed *Mass* by bloggers and news stations, he was once frail and weak, a peon forever stepped on but, after experimental growth hormone treatments, grew to something deadly. Strong-arm robbery wasn't enough for his rage and his need for power so he began tearing buildings down bare handed, eventually charging the city large fees to stop the destruction. Tranquilizer darts, shot from personal on-sight guards, punctured Mass's tough exterior before he shrunk back down; his deep growl becoming a whimper.

Both these two, and lots more, brought in by Agent Phoenix and others of the Agency. Lannerman grew increasingly nervous seeing these caged animals, some looking at him with disapproval and some looking at him with promise, but all with curiosity. Other prisoners were being transferred to different wings as The Mailman was being brought through. They'd almost reached the end of the great hall when Baxter Combs was coming through with his own pair of guards. Combs stopped and eyed the newbie up and down.

"Huh, amateur..." Baxter scoffed and shook his head.

"That's enough. Keep it moving, Combs." The guard instructed.

"You, too. Go." Lannerman's guards told him.

The villains parted and were taken to their sectors. The cells of various offenders had a different response to the sight of Combs, with a good deal of them averting their eyes.

Victor sat at home grading papers with a glass of wine. Smooth jazz played on the overhead. He nursed his drink and checked incorrect answers while, instead of blunt red strikes, he wrote notes on the page explaining *why* they were wrong. Occasionally he'd write notes to the ace writers to congratulate them. Victor looked at the shortening stack and knew he'd be finished soon.

The clock revealed it to be late; not too late, but late enough to make him worry about Tobin. Late nights usually ended with his husband coming through the front door looking worse for wear. Bruised, bloodied, and battle-worn. Over a bag of ice and a stiff drink, Victor had asked him why he has to go to such extremes. Tobin's response was always the same: to catch them you have to speed up. He told Victor that he didn't want a *chance* at catching them, he wanted to lock them up; and to do that meant having to step it up beyond his colleagues at the Agency. Victor had seen his husband transform from patriotic, by-the-book agent to a hardened law machine; quickly rising to the top in his field.

Of course Mr. Louis-Phoenix had an inkling early on in Tobin's metamorphosis that for all the good he'd done, he would have twice as many enemies. Tobin, once safe and tame, was now under fire on a regular basis, never giving up. The bigger and badder the suspect was, Tobin worked that much harder. Through the years, Victor had often felt as if he was playing second fiddle to the agent's subjects. The nightmares, the near-death experiences, the fighting, the death - they took up space in his life, and Victor was uncomfortable with the growing crowd. Arguments between them would usually end with an interrupting phone call and a fast exit.

He graded his last paper before finishing off his glass of wine. The papers were stacked neatly and placed in a folder before being relocated to his bag. Victor stretched and rubbed his neck when the doorbell rang. With Tobin's phone call earlier, along with the news stream of the bombings, Victor was hesitant about answering the door. It rang once more followed by a knocking. His heart skipped a beat and he feared the worst; beyond that of a villainous fiend popping up, the thought of an agent bringing the news that Tobin had finally met his match.

"Hello? Who is it?" Victor asked, stepping forward.

"Pizza." A muffled voice said.

"I didn't order any pizza."

"Special delivery."

"Delivery?" He asked aloud and to himself.

He took a deep breath and opened the door just a crack to find Tobin Phoenix holding a pizza box with a sly grin across his face. Victor opened the door fully while both relieved and slightly perturbed.

"Someone in need of a pizza with extra...me?" Tobin playfully winked and blew a kiss.

"Oh, I don't know, pizza boy, my husband should be home any minute now." He leaned against the door frame and crossed his arms.

"I'm sure he wouldn't mind if I came in for a slice."

"I don't know, he's a bit of a bad ass."

"Oh really?" Tobin stepped closer.

"Yeah." Victor nodded.

"I'm sure I could take him."

He held the pizza to the side and got closer. Victor edged forward.

"Think so, huh?"

"Yeah..."

They came together in a strong, passionate kiss, separating only briefly.

"You know you had me nervous." Victor punched his arm lightly.

"There's nothing to be nervous about. I got you."

"Yeah?" He asked with a smile.

"Yeah." They kissed again.

"Let's go in, secret agent man."

The two enjoyed their pizza and end of the day conversation, keeping topics light for the most part. Victor wanted to ask about the Mailman and the bombings, but thought against it. Instead, they talked about Victor's day teaching and grading assignments and Agent Martinie's stomach bug. In the early days, Tobin would tell everything of his day, every punch and pull of the trigger as well as any tea he'd heard while on the job. As things got heavier, Agent Phoenix decided to leave work at work the best he could, figuring it would keep Victor safer and less stressed. When he did finally speak on the day, Tobin summed up Lannerman's vengeful exploits briefly, giving quick facts and leaving out the slight slugfest the two engaged in. Regardless of the fighting not being mentioned or detailed, Victor could tell by the soreness and the light bruising how the capture of the bomber went down.

When the last slice was consumed, they threw the box away and retreated to the bedroom. Tobin stripped out of his uniform while Victor watched, unbeknownst to him. He didn't know why but the agent's battle scars made him all the more sexier, an added ruggedness to his already handsome figure.

"I'm jumping in the shower."

"Don't be too long." Victor grinned.

"A scrub down, a rinse, and I'm out."

Victor nodded and Tobin disappeared into the bathroom off of the bedroom. He showered and stretched his aching muscles, mentally going over the events of the day. Tobin wondered if Lannerman would've continued after his revenge mission was complete, having tasted the power of causing such great fear in a short amount of time. He'd never know and he was fine not knowing. Agent Phoenix didn't get the chance to ask the Mailman about his tech but had his team look into it. If the technology used in those envelopes would be shared, well, he didn't want to think about the mess he'd have to clean up.

His wounds, though merely surface, hurt when washing them, but he toughed through it. The constant pain inflicted on him pushed him further. It was one of the main things that drove him. To be able to take damage from his enemies and continue in full force to fight for justice would always be one of his greatest assets. He rinsed off, both the soap and his incessant thoughts, and stepped out of the shower. Upon wiping the steam from the mirror he saw his tattered exterior. Some scars weren't visible to anyone but him. The years of fighting and the creeps kept coming in different forms, from The Feeder to Baxter and everyone in between. Wondering if the eternal fight was worth it or not wasn't in his DNA. What did cross his mind, however, was the fear that Victor would tire of the danger, the late nights, and the physical toll it was taking on his husband. Tobin loved him more than anything but feared he'd inadvertently been pushing him away.

He dried off and opened the door to a candlelit bedroom. Victor was nude and bent over the bed, presenting. Despite the soreness, Tobin was instantly erect. Victor looked back at him.

"Figured after a hard day you could use some winding down."

Tobin smiled and threw his towel to the side and stepped up to his man.

The prisoners at Bellview were having a less enjoyable time. William Lannerman sat on his bed even more nervous than when he was brought in. The sound of screams and laughter overlapped one another to a painful cackle. The anger echoing through the corridors riled him up. He quickly remembered the one that got away. Cheryl Barton, out there living a lie. A story only she and her partners in the firm knew. He vowed to avenge his family and knowing she's out there fueled him all the more.

Manfred Peltzer, *Red Talon*, sat in his cage of a cell tapping on the bars. Along with a skin condition which reddens his body, he'd surgically implanted large hook-like blades into his forearms. The talons had grafted to his skeleton by the time of his capture, so the guards had them wrapped and padded. Still he taps them on the bars.

Known only as *Venus*, she sat in the middle of her cell, rocking back and forth while periodically counting the walls. She played innocent, kind, but before being apprehended she would lure men in, sleep with them, and eventually, eat them.

Baxter Combs stood scraping the metallic art on his arms along the walls. The sound was loud even with the chaotic audio space.

Others throughout sang their woeful song, cursed the Agency, and vowed to escape. One rarely ever did. But Baxter was determined. His mind raced with endless possibilities.

The candles had burned down and the coitus was finished. Tobin sat in the bed with his arm around Victor. They enjoyed the peace and quiet. No need to rush anywhere, they were where they needed to be.

"What are you thinking about?" Tobin asked.

"Well, part of me wants to know more about what happens at work, when you're out on the job, but the rest of me fears what I'd find."

"How so?"

"It's just, I worry enough as it is without the details. As much as I *do* know, I'm sure finding out any extra would give me nightmares... But I feel this need to know more of you."

"Vic, we've been married for years. We *know* each other."

"I know that. I get that. It's just I want to know *all* of you. The Agency's like this no signal area in our life. I've always believed that if you want to get closer with someone, to know them better, then you get to know their work. I mean, you've been to the university. You know who I am here but also through what I do."

A silent moment passed as Tobin thought about what he was saying. Victor just assumed let it go as what he was requesting might actually be against Agency policy.

"I'll tell you what," Tobin started, "Why don't you come to work with me. Just office stuff, nothing crazy. Just a visit and you can see more of what I do. What do you say?"

"I-I'm shocked. Yes, I'd love to."

"We'll get you a visitor's pass."

"Sounds good. I'm excited."

They kissed and turned off the bedside lamp.

"Goodnight. I love you."

"Goodnight, babe. I love you too."

Tobin and Victor curled up in the darkness and drifted asleep.

Agent Phoenix sat in his office while tech support looked over his ammo clip charging panel.

"I'm sorry, sir, but I don't see anything wrong with it." Regardless, he continued inspecting.

"Well there's gotta be something. I had a full charge and the clip was short."

"Might've been a faulty clip. A lemon from the factory."

"I'd used it before with no trouble."

"Ah, here it is. You got a port shorted out."

He reached into his tool bag to find the necessary tools before unscrewing the panel base. Third port from the left. The yellow wire had burn marks. He began to rewire when Agent Brick rushed into the office, almost crashing into the man.

"Phoenix! It's Baxter, he's escaped!"

No words came to Agent Phoenix, only the urge to move. He snatched his gun and clips and dashed out of the office.

"We don't have eyes on him yet." Brick said, following him out of the building.

Agent Phoenix stopped at his cruiser, opened the door, and turned back.

"Get to Bellview and see how he got out."

"Where are you going?"

"I gotta get to Victor." Phoenix got in and immediately sped off.

Victor's class had just let out and he had some time before the next. He erased the whiteboard and sat down to prep his next lesson plan when he heard the door.

"Next class isn't for a while." He said, head still in his planner.

The door shut and clunking footsteps were audible. Victor looked up, at first casually but soon gasped. His pen dropped from his hand as he shook. He recognized the man standing before him in a bloodied prison jumpsuit. The deranged look in his eyes and the salivating grin made Victor's skin crawl.

Agent Phoenix flew down the streets, knowing the routes to the university well. He spun the Agency issued craft hard to the left down a side street, nearly causing a wreck behind him, and floored it. He wouldn't get very far along as his engine sputtered and popped before slowing to an unwanted stop.

"What the...? C'mon, not now damn it!" Phoenix yelled, slamming his fists on the wheel.

He tried it again but it was no use. The cruiser had powered down completely with the door having to be forced open before he got out. In this particular instance Phoenix didn't care about the repercussions of leaving an official vehicle and set out on foot. The more he ran, the longer the streets seemed to stretch, furthering his destination. Everything contorted and everyone to either side of him in passing came across as suspicious and grew more so. Phoenix fought hard to fully tune out the strange new city of suspects and to press on without questioning or busting them. His blinders helped him stay focused, even if no one saw it. Sweat ran from his pores, and his heartbeat galloped. His legs were rubbery, and his breath was shortening. Agent Phoenix stopped and looked around, finding himself lost. In a panic he wondered if he'd ever make it, when the university materialized.

He stormed inside to find its halls vacant, echoing with his panting.

"Victor!" He screamed as his voice rippled through the air.

He could hear *something*. A struggle. Phoenix ran down the halls noticing the rooms to his sides no longer contained numbers or any other identifying attributes, just blank doors. There, at the end of the hall, a lone door was open with its light shining into the darkened corridor. The struggle was becoming louder the closer the agent got. Agent Phoenix ran and *dove* through the open doorway, rolling upon hitting the floor.

"Always the entrance maker." Baxter laughed.

Phoenix stood and reached for his pistol slowly upon seeing Victor held captive between them.

"Vic, I got you. It's gonna be okay." Tobin told him.

Victor nervously nodded before Baxter gripped his neck tighter.

"Baxter,"

"Blah blah blah. Let him go, this is between us and he's innocent." Combs sarcastically said. "Truth is, Agent Phoenix, *you* put him here."

His lip snarled and he drew fast, aimed right at Baxter's face, and squeezed the trigger to sparks and nothing else. A brief light emitted from the barrel but no blast.

"No, what the-?"

He stopped, stunned, and shook the pistol, slapping it before trying again to no avail. Baxter laughed heartily.

"Time's up, Phoenix."

Baxter plunged his dagger through Victor's back and through his chest. Tobin screamed and lunged for his love but couldn't move. He looked down to find his feet fused to the floor. Victor's body was thrown to the floor in front of his husband.

"Don't worry, Phoenix. I got you." Baxter laughed and faded.

Victor lay dead. Baxter gone. Agent Phoenix wept.

Tobin jolted awake with sharp breaths. Victor instantly shot up to console him.

"It's okay. It's okay."

Tobin began to realize it was only a nightmare as Vic held him close.

"Just a bad dream."

Tobin sat up, rubbed his face, and got out of bed.

"Where are you going, babe?" Victor sleepily asked.

"Just gonna get up. There's no way in hell I'm getting back to sleep. You get your rest though, try to go back to sleep."

Tobin leaned forward and kissed Victor's forehead. He left the room, closing the door quietly.

He leaned up against the kitchen counter waiting for the coffee to brew. Early morning blues, he wrestled with his dream and all it entailed. The conversation about Victor visiting work returned in his head. He thought after the nightmare that it might be a good idea. Tobin poured the coffee as its billowing steam showed him his malfunctioning pistol and *its* steam. He grabbed his phone and hoped that the night crew weren't on break.

"Agent Phoenix to third shift tech support."

"Patching you through, sir."

"Tech here, Agent."

"Yes, I need you to check my ammo charger base and the clip ports."

"Been having issues with your clips?"

"No, just... Just call it a hunch."

"Copy that. I'll get on it."

"Thanks."

Tobin ended the call and sat down at the table. The image of Victor dying kept replaying on a loop. He tried to let the scenario play again while trying to control it but his legs still wouldn't move and Vic still died. He couldn't alter the dream but created a revenge fantasy to where he caught Baxter and finally killed him once and for all. The vision broke with hands on his shoulders. He jerked slightly.

"It's just me." Victor said, kissing the side of his head and rubbing his shoulders. "You wanna talk about it?"

"No. Sorry." Tobin shook his head. "Sorry I woke you."

"You don't have to apologize. You can't control it." Victor walked over to get his own coffee.

"I've tried." He sipped. "It's like I don't know how to keep it but I don't know how to let it go."

"You just need a break from everything." Vic sat down beside him. "You bag one creep after the next after the next. It's just wearing on you. I mean, let Martinie go it alone once in a while and take time off."

Tobin thought about it but also knew it was almost time to get ready for work. Whether or not Martinie was over his bug is something he'd find out once he got to the office. He wondered if he'd even be able to enjoy time off or if he'd simply be waiting for something to hit the fan, causing him to spring into action. Evil was always lurking and justice always had to be ready.

A NIGHT OUT

IT WAS a dark night and the streets of Carbine City seemed vacant. The neon glow of holographic advertisements lit where streetlights wouldn't reach. The shadows of the city were thick and inky black. The same shadows used to aid criminals in hiding but that didn't matter anymore. They came when they pleased. Most of them wanted an audience to their already devious acts. With the likes of The Feeder, The Mailman, and Baxter Combs acting in broad daylight, the night held no more of a threat than an average afternoon. Foot traffic was light. Cabs picked up and dropped off. Buses ran their usual routes. The alleys were Carbine City's blind spots.

Agent Martinie entered and immediately began inspecting his surroundings. A call led him to the dark alley. He walked slowly, scanning the shadows for the reason for the distress call. He pulled his weapon from its holster. Cans rattled. He spun quickly with aim. An old woman pushed a shopping cart of old soda cans. She stopped abruptly and threw her hands up. He lowered his gun, held up his hand, and nodded his apology. She moved on with a breath of relief and picked up more stray cans along the way. Martinie turned the corner to an empty lot. Few cars stayed parked awaiting their owners while a couple sat with cold, dead engines. Steam rose from vents.

The backdoor to the building in back of the lot slung open and the agent's pistol came up. Laughing coworkers came out amidst conversation and turned and locked the door. They didn't see Martinie before his weapon lowered. They smiled at him and said their goodnights to each other. The cars left the lot but Martinie stayed alert. Behind him a dumpster was thrown against a wall cracking the brick beneath. He spun around sharply to find a being in the shadows. It stepped out, massive and draped in the same black that made up such shadows. Its hands gripped the sides of the dumpster with its fingers digging into the metal. Martinie's hands gripped the pistol in return while ordering it to stop it. Needless to say, the thing didn't comply. He couldn't make out whether the being was male or female but he knew it blended into the darkness easily, was quite large, and was strong as it lifted the dumpster above its head. The agent shot several rounds into the dumpster, freeing it from the thing's grasp. The dark figure rushed Martinie and he fired. Swiftly, it dodged left and right avoiding the blasts. It sprung up and dove down upon the agent. He fell back and shot frantically as the being blew apart in shadowy wisps.

Martinie was relieved as his stilted breathing showed. The wisps of what was left of it had vanished and he stood up and dusted himself off. In the corner of his eye he saw another dark figure, one more tangible. He turned to see a *ninja* standing on one of the dead cars. Martinie never heard it. The ninja unveiled a sword from the sheath on his back. Another jumped down to join him and brandished his blade as well. Their sharp, piercing eyes were the only details standing out to the agent. One jumped down while the other flipped over and behind Agent Martinie and he found himself betwixt two deadly killers waiting to strike. He tried to keep his gun from trembling. He drew quickly but didn't get a shot off as the sword cut the piece in half. Without his weapon he understood he had to rely on his hand-to-hand training. The first ninja stabbed the point of his blade at him but he dodged just in time and the sword cut his uniform. The second swiped his sword to which Martinie ducked, narrowly escaping beheading. Severed hair ends drifted to the lot beneath.

They stalked their prey, circling him while twirling their weapons. Martinie's heart raced and his nerves jumped. They attacked! He dodged, punched, and kicked them. They struck back with kicks of fury and swipes of the sword. Martinie endured painful stabs and cuts but was getting better at seeing a pattern, a rhythm, and began avoiding further maneuvers. He was still taking a beating and they continued to throw blows. He watched one's kicking pattern and the other's swordsman pattern. He tried to memorize it while taking nicks and kicks to the body and head. Now! He kicked one back and instantly ducked down. The ninja came back with a roundhouse while his partner chopped and sliced forward, cutting off his leg. Martinie caught it. While the legless grabbed at his bloody stump, the agent hit the other's hand with his leg, sending the sword back at its handler. He swung it again, finally driving the blade the rest of the way into his neck. Both ninjas dropped and Martinie threw the severed leg down joining them. He leaned on the car in pure exhaustion.

The bodies of the black clad ninjas were soon no more. Martinie recouped, coughed, and got a short stretch in when he heard a child's laughter followed by a woman's. A couple came up through the alley and into the lot. They carried on with conversation until they saw Martinie.

"Agent." The man greeted them upon seeing his attire.

They headed for the last parked car with life left in it. Upon trying to unlock the door, bright blasts shot forth from the alleyway. The family screamed and the man did his best to cover his wife and child. Thugs in torn camouflage and jeans draped in chains walked up wielding cybernetic cannons.

"C'mon!" Martinie yelled, ushering the family behind the car.

The three men moved forward shooting up the vehicle while the agent tried to keep the family safe.

"Stay down." He told them.

He looked over the car to find the pierced faces of anger and deviance. The fingers of the hoods stayed on the triggers and the weapons pulsed pushing lasers sharply against the car, leaving it in tatters the more they fired. Glass breaking, metal denting and tearing, the parents screamed and cried covering their child. Martinie thought quickly on what to do since his firearm was destroyed. One more fast peek around the car almost got Martinie's head blown off. He retracted it just in time but they were getting closer. He looked around him for anything of use only to find loose rocks and broken pieces of asphalt. He grabbed the biggest piece of broken parking lot he could and waited in between shots fired. Martinie sprung up and launched the rock overhead, hitting the man to the far right. The blunt hit knocked his weapon over, shooting his comrade to his right. Two down, one to go, but the power blasts kept coming. Martinie knew never to bring a knife to a high-powered gunfight but his resources were depleted so he pulled the dagger from his boot. The other two were stirring around and working their way back up. There was a brief pause in the firing and Martinie saw his opportunity. He shot up and marked his target. He and the gunman locked eyes before he threw the knife with fierce precision. Direct hit, the blade landed square in the barrel before the trigger was pulled. Martinie ducked back down to shield the family. The power surged and the cannon exploded, annihilating the three thugs.

Agent Martinie stepped out from behind the car now riddled with holes and burn spots. Inspecting the scene he found no trace of the three men.

"It's alright. They're gone."

He didn't hear anything of the family. He walked back to assure them that all was fine to see they had vanished as well. Behind him, across the lot, steam had ceased rising from the vent and was replaced by an orange gel protruding from the grate. Martinie picked up half of his pistol and looked at the clean cut.

"Damn it."

He threw it down as the grate *popped* off the vent and flew through the air. The agent jumped and his view shot over to find a gigantic, gelatinous, orange slug-like creature slithering out of the vent.

"What in the..."

After the initial shock, he grabbed the loose stones he'd seen prior and threw them at the slimy beast. The rocks made contact but sunk into its body. Martinie jumped up on one of the broken down cars. It dragged itself along the ground leaving a slug trail behind it. It edged closer as its tongue slid out of the wide hole at the end of its body and pulsated, wagging around tasting. Martinie waited, watching it squirm. A ball bounced down the alley and rolled into the vicinity.

"Get back here, boy. Leave the damn ball."

It turned its attention to the dog running in to retrieve the ball. A man followed, old with a limp in heavily stained clothing.

"C'mon now, playtime's over."

The dog stopped, no longer caring about the ball. He bared his teeth and growled.

"What're you gettin' into now?" The man asked from the dark

alley.

The thing's tongue whipped out and snatched the dog by its front legs. Its yelp echoed between the walls. Martinie watched as it began to drag it in screaming. He jumped down from the car and kicked and stomped at the beast. His boots struck with a splat of orange sludge but it remolded soon after. It took the dog into its mouth as its barking and whimpering muffled.

"Holy Moses!" The old man yelled, upon seeing the image of a creature eating his dog while being kicked by an agent.

The man approached the area as his dog was completely swallowed whole. Martinie stopped kicking the creature when he saw the old man. Its body trembled while digesting the canine. Agent Martinie leapt over the grimy thing to the civilian.

"My dog!"

"Let's get you out of here!"

Martinie led him back through the alley.

The old man pixelated and disappeared. The alley and lot did the same. The orange slug belched and faded soon after. The city surrounding quickly revealed itself as black and chrome walls. Martinie looked up and shrugged.

"Well?"

"Did great, agent. You're clear." The voice said over the speaker.

The worker typed up the results along with notes while Agent Phoenix, Agent Brick, and Victor watched from an enclosed skyrise.

"You guys put on a show for every visitor?" Victor asked.

"No," Phoenix chuckled, "This is just a short refresher training simulator for whenever an agent's been out sick or injured."

"This is just a *short* training?"

"Yep." Agent Brick nodded. "The regular training mod is an all-day affair. This is just a select few to test abilities that could possibly be off. Our Agent Phoenix is the only one to ace it upon every return."

Victor was impressed. Tobin smiled.

"I thought Martinie did pretty good. What did you do differently?" Victor asked.

"I just did some things sooner and made sure I didn't lose my weapon."

"And most importantly, he saved the dog." Brick laughed and patted Tobin's chest.

"So... What was that thing?" Victor pointed beyond the glass where the creature once was.

The agents laughed.

"That's Mona. We created her for the sim." Tobin said. "Don't worry, those things don't exist."

"Oh! Whew. You had me wondering." Victor snickered.

Martinie entered the room.

"Good job, agent. You picked up on patterns and you thought quickly." Agent Brick said.

"Thanks, guys. Agent Phoenix, how did you beat that last...thing?"

"I grabbed the dog and ran up the car. It ate the car and it weighed it down until I got the old man out." Agent Phoenix answered. "You can't beat it. The point of that segment is to get the civilian to safety and you did just that."

"Well, guys, I have a class to get to." Victor said looking at his watch.

"We better get to it around here too." Agent Brick said and began walking away with Martinie.

"See ya, Victor." Martinie said.

"Bye."

"Well, now you got to see a little bit of my work in a safer way."

"It was exciting. Is it always like *that* when you go out."

"Sometimes it's pretty standard, but often times it's worse because it's real."

"Be safe out there, agent. I gotta get going."

"Alright, you be safe too."

They kissed and Victor left. Tobin looked down through the glass at the empty training room, wishing his real villains were more like the simulation.

"Everything all right, sir?" The man at the computer asked.

"Yeah, just...thinking..."

"Thinking about giving it a shot? Beating your record?" The worker grinned.

"No. Not today." Agent Phoenix exited.

The restaurant was lit by gold and red hues. Chandeliers hung with sharp twinkling and the candles at each table burned bright, the edges of their lights' reach almost touching in the middle. Waiters brought out steaming hot plates to tables of impressed diners. Wine flowed and bread was broken. Laughter and conversation filled the soundscape.

"Phoenix, party of four." The hostess called.

Tobin and Victor entered the dining area with Agent Martinie and his wife. Despite his active and dangerous career, Joshua Martinie was an average, normal man, dressed in a suit and tie. His wife Katie was pretty, barely in the agent's league, wearing a red dress with her blonde hair down. Tobin pulled Victor's chair out for him as did Joshua for Katie. They sat down and were greeted instantly.

"Welcome to Culver Strada. Can I start you off with some drinks?"

They mulled it over and ordered their drinks. The waiter told them how fast he'd return.

"So how long have you been in Carbine City?" Victor asked Katie and her husband.

"Not long. We moved here after he graduated from the academy." Katie answered.

"We love it here." Joshua nodded. Katie agreed.

"We've been here a while." Tobin said.

"It's a wonderful place but it seems to be a hub for trouble." Katie said concerned.

"There are some nutjobs out there but it's no different than anywhere else. I read a piece today, in Echoville there was this big woman in some kind of armor. Think they called her WarMother or something. She had like a Viking helmet with cannons. These cases are everywhere. Carbine City is fantastic, it's our home. Plus we got *these* guys protecting us." Victor said.

"Yeah we do!" Katie and Victor clinked glasses.

Tobin and Joshua shared a warming smile.

"Here you are." The waiter returned with a tray of their ordered drinks circling a bottle of wine. He served their individual drinks before holding up the bottle. "A little something from the owner. Miss Harreth sends her regards."

He set the bottle down and left. The table of four smiled at each other.

"Will you look at that?" Tobin looked over the wine.

"Enjoying the perks of your fanbase?" Victor grinned.

"I may have helped her out a little."

"A little? He saved her life!" Martinie said sounding like an excited child. He looked at Katie. "Her husband was an amateur bodybuilder. Had anger issues that were only getting worse with his steroid use. But it also wasn't helping his multiple personalities. One of these other people in him was a jealous wife. She'd see Miss Harreth and go berserk. Damn near killed her by the time we showed up."

"I took a beating of a lifetime." Tobin shook his head and took a drink.

Katie listened with wide eyes and a dropped jaw while Victor had heard it all before.

"Yeah but you got him though and she's obviously grateful." Joshua added.

"That's not always the case." Victor said with the thought in mind of all his husband does and the little gratitude he receives.

"But enough of all that. Tonight's a night off." Tobin raised his glass and the others followed.

Baxter Combs sat in his cell watching the patterns of which the guards walked, counted the time intervals, and eyed each prisoner brought in. The airspace was rich with violent screams and wild cackles. It all brought a smile to Baxter's face. He could almost tell who the screams belonged to as well as who was causing them. Some of the other inmates had a history with Combs while others were new to the game. Few impressed him as most of these were no more than dime store hoods compared to his high standards of villainy. He waited for his moment, counting steps and scraping the metal on his skin against the bars that held him. His rage swelled within him as he bided his time.

"So then Martinie's hanging out of the car trying to get the guy to stop." Tobin laughed.

"The guy wouldn't pull over!" Joshua said.

The four laughed together. The time was spent telling stories while intermittently eating their meal.

"Hell, I'll take my job over Vic's any day."

"Is it hard?" Katie asked Victor.

"It's not hard. Just tedious, monotonous. Sometimes it's like I'm up there talking just to talk."

"I'm sure you're reaching them." Katie assured him.

"That's what I keep telling him." Tobin said in between bites.

"I loved my teachers." Katie said.

"Sadly, I wasn't the best of students." Joshua winced.

"Well you probably didn't have a teacher like Victor." Katie smiled.

"That's sweet. Thank you."

"I agree." Tobin added. "It just takes one good teacher to turn the learning experience around."

"That's a lot of pressure, babe."

"Well I stand by it. You're incredible."

"Awww you guys are so *cute*." Katie gushed. "How come you never say that stuff to me?" She nudged her husband.

They all looked at him. He laughed, flabbergasted.

"What? I tell you you're incredible all the time!"

"I know. He does." She told them. "He's great."

"I know he's a hell of a partner." Tobin said.

The agents shared a look and a slight glass raise. There was a break in conversation allowing everyone to eat.

"So what happened to your last partner?" Katie asked after wiping her mouth with her napkin.

Tobin and Victor looked at each other.

"Babe..." Joshua said.

"Sorry, I was just curious." She said seeing the looks on their faces.

"No, you're fine." Victor assured her.

"It's a dangerous job and sometimes bad things happen. We went out on the job one day and I came back alone. I still think having to tell his family was harder than losing him." Tobin informed them.

"Tobin was a wreck after his death."

"I wasn't fast enough and he wasn't alert to his surroundings. Luckily Martinie here has proven to be sharp as a tack. Always alert, always on it." Tobin said, just barely alleviating Katie's fears.

"Well..." Katie thought to herself and looked at Joshua.

A loud crash rang out in the front of the restaurant followed by an equally loud commotion. The agents leapt up and rushed to investigate. Victor sighed while Katie sat more confused. The two shared a look conveying something only spouses of lawmen could understand. Victor leaned in.

"Does Martinie, er, Joshua ever have nightmares? Like does the job ever get to him?"

Katie was lost on the question and what it might mean for the future of his mental health.

"No, not that I'm aware of. He sleeps pretty sound." She answered.

Tobin and Joshua returned and sat down.

"Someone hit a parked car and then the front window of the place next door. No one's hurt." Tobin explained.

"Never thought I'd be happy to say it's *just* a car accident." Joshua chuckled inappropriately before seeing his wife's disapproving look.

"Who's up for dessert?" Tobin asked.

Victor and Katie shared that look once more.

The look Victor and Katie shared was one every agent's spouse had worn at one time or another. The Carbine City Agency had seen its fair share of widows throughout its history. CCPD were doing a fine job in keeping the city safe but weren't trained for what was ahead. They had thwarted thieves and drug dealers, caught killers and abusive husbands. But the tide had turned as small problems became big problems. The advancing technology of the world was spreading and once it was in the hands of those who once dwelled in the shadows of Carbine City, things changed. Common criminals became super villains overnight. Crime ruled over justice. The people were terrified. The police were at a loss. High-powered thugs were the talk of the city and the media ate it up. Others wanted what they had. The spotlight, the ability to rule with fear, the *power*. Once quiet citizens exposed hidden abnormalities - biological mutations or extra-human abilities - to get ahead in the crime industry, and business was booming.

There had come a time when the rate of villains reported equaled up to one in every household. The police managed to make some staying arrests but not very many. The disease spread until a new order was passed down. The CCPD had to step aside as extensively trained commandos came in, they were called Agents. Nobody saw the construction of the headquarters, the Base. The building was put up fast and efficiently, the Carbine City Agency. These Agencies had been showing up sporadically around the globe. The man in charge was Agency Director Salvatore Wachowski, a young man whose drive and abilities were far superior to his cohorts. To the present, the only records Agent Phoenix hadn't broken belonged to Director Wachowski. The crime rate dropped dramatically after the agents went to work. The territorial police and the new Agency butted heads but the force was reminded of the pecking order, and not to mention the differential in skill level.

The two sects eventually became cordial. New waves of fresh

agents came through from the academy; an establishment so secretive that the students themselves don't know its location. They were selected, tested, and transferred blindfolded.

Director Wachowski had come back from the field but something was changed. While he continued his role in the Agency, he had become reclusive and without the desire to go out on cases. Agents had rarely seen or heard him since. Two generations of recruits later and Agent Phoenix had become what the Director once was. Though the two never met, Phoenix looked up to him and his accomplishments in the Agency. While the number of agents in the field grew, so did that of the outlaws. With Wachowski no longer taking on missions, the agents did their best fending off the evils of Carbine City. The city foes were resilient.

Other Agency locations saw significant drops in crime that would rarely spike back up as Carbine City saw new villains rise. For every Agent Phoenix, there was a Baxter Combs. They wanted power, money, and control. To some of the villainous scum the arrival of an agent meant an added competition, another hurdle - the *biggest* hurdle - between them and their goal of destruction and domination. To match the increasing waves of terror the Agents were in constant training. From advanced target practice to combat training, from driving to mental tests. A period of meditation was required after training. The agents studied the criminals, their methods, their habits.

While the average thief or killer would be sent to Carbine City Penitentiary, those that the Agency sought out were detained in a separate location. Bellview was a former mental institution, condemned before the Agency arrived. They remodeled it and since then it's been their storage facility for evil doers. Security kept a watchful eye on their inmates. The more of them that were brought in, the safer the city became. But just like weeds, more sprouted, and agents went out to tend to their garden that was Carbine City.

JOYRIDE

THE AGENCY cruiser stopped at the sign and Agent Phoenix checked his monitor.

"You all right? You seem a little off lately." Agent Martinie asked.

While his fingers typed his eyes peered over.

"I don't mean *off*-off. You're doing a hell of a job." Martinie nervously rambled. "I mean there seems to be something up."

"I'm fine. Just trouble sleeping is all."

"You've been in the field a long time. Job getting to you?"

"What do you say we get to work, Agent?" Phoenix suggested.

Martinie nodded and threw out any more personal questions.

"This morning a cruiser was reported missing from the Agency garage."

"Couldn't an agent have just taken it out on the beat?" Martinie asked, not finding anything suspicious in the information.

"There was nothing in the logs. It wasn't signed out."

"Maybe they just forgot?"

"It's not likely. The craft's tracking code isn't coming up. No agents have been unaccounted for."

"Why don't they just look at the security files?"

"All footage recorded in the last twenty four hours has been blacked out."

"Blacked out?"

"My guess is, deleted."

"Who could steal an Agency vehicle?"

"That's what we're going to find out. Let's roll."

The vehicle accelerated but kept the speed down as they began their hunt. They each kept an eye out for other Agency crafts on the road as well as who was driving them. Another cruiser passed them with an agent behind the wheel. He and Phoenix gave each other a nod in passing.

"Well that one's clear." Martinie said, scanning the streets.

"We'll do a quick pass through the city and then we'll ask around. For all we know it's abandoned somewhere."

"Or stripped for parts." Martinie threw out.

"Well, let's hope that's not the case. We don't need this kind of equipment on the streets in untrained hands."

They searched the streets of Carbine City. Mundane lives were lived out. Always on the move. To work, from work. Shopping. Endless shopping. Much like the agents' watchful eyes, a homeless man sat outside an alley on a small crate watching the city move around him.

"Why don't we ask him? He might've seen something." Martinie suggested.

"Could have. Looks like he's been at it a while."

They pulled up to the curb and parked.

"Alright, Martinie, this one's yours."

"Yes sir."

The man watched the cruiser with nervous eyes but tried not to stare. The doors opened and he averted his eyes completely, turning to the side in his seat. Agents Phoenix and Martinie stepped out. Martinie casually approached the man with Phoenix close behind. The man fidgeted where he sat.

"Excuse me." Agent Martinie started.

"I don't know nothin'!"

"We just want to ask you a question."

"I didn't do nothin', didn't see nothin'!" The man's words whistled through his missing teeth.

As the agents stepped closer the man stood, picking up his stool of a crate, and walked into the alley.

"I got nothin' for ya! Go away!" He yelled, waving them off.

"Good job, agent, you scared him off." Phoenix said casually.

Martinie followed. Phoenix looked side to side before joining them. A couple of other alley-dwellers exited swiftly upon seeing the agents. The two men in uniform walked in without aggression.

"We're not gonna hurt you. We just have some questions."

He turned back to see Agent Phoenix reach in his belt. The thin, shabby looking man in rags froze and trembled. Martinie looked over to Phoenix who removed a piece of gum. He opened it and popped it in his mouth and shrugged at his partner. Martinie took the man's fear as an advantage.

"Look," he approached him, "We just want to inquire about something you may have seen. You're not a target or a suspect. Just looking for a little help." Agent Martinie held his hands out as if approaching a frightened animal.

"You're not here to kill me? You're not assassins?" The man questioned with bug eyes.

Phoenix rolled his eyes. Martinie sighed.

"You look like you've been doing some people watching. Seen any vehicles you may remember?"

"Wh-what?"

"Vehicles that pass by the alley."

"Oh, I see 'em all the time. Some real beauties out there. I used to own a 2049 Blackbird. She was a classic. She had a duel steam engine that would-"

"Have you seen any Agency vehicles pass by, last night or this morning?"

"Always see 'em. You boys run this city."

"If only..." Phoenix muttered.

"There was one tear-assin' through here last night. Must've been on the hunt."

"Did you see who was driving? Can you describe them?"

"I can't see nothin' through that damn tint. I watched in hopes for some action but couldn't see who they were chasin'. Just took off like a bat outta hell."

"Which way did they go?"

"I don't really remember. I may have had a little drink." He said, barely holding his thumb and fingertip apart.

"Drunks don't usually make good eyewitnesses, Martinie." Phoenix said quietly.

"Is there anything you can remember about it? What time it was? Anything?" The agent continued.

"Uh..." The man scratched his head, trying hard to find

something in his colander of memory.

"Forget it, agent. That vehicle could've been any one of ours. We don't have a chance of knowing that it was the stolen craft."

"Hey man, I don't steal nothin'." He threw his arms up.

"Yeah, yeah, you're free to go. We're done here." Phoenix patted his partner's arm and they began to walk away.

"So, so, that's it?" Their alley man wondered aloud.

"That's it. Thank you for your cooperation."

They walked back to their cruiser, both looking around them. Most civilians avoided eye contact and passed well around the two. They listened for any engine accelerations in their area. A calm day like any other.

"And the search continues..."

They got in and Phoenix checked his monitors once more.

"Still not coming up."

"Where to next?" Martinie asked.

"Not a drunken homeless man." Phoenix smirked.

Martinie returned the look and nodded. Their vehicle left the curb. They drove and watched the city buzzing with life. Upon seeing the Agency craft, anybody shoving their way through the stream of traffic on the sidewalk calmed and walked casually; those cutting through the handicap lane also stuck to their designated space. Possible snatchers watched women in front of them with their purses, considering how easy it would be, until the agents' cruiser came by. They quickly rethought the trade of taking a beating from an agent for a possibility that something worthwhile might be in said purse. Commuters passed through more holographic advertisements that lit the city even in the bright light of day. Vehicles passed with no signs of suspicion but Phoenix still examined them in passing. He kept an eye on the monitor for the missing cruiser while Martinie watched the city inhabitants move about, wondering what their intentions were. They turned the corner and another Agency cruiser was parked up ahead to the left. Phoenix pulled up alongside.

Phoenix and Martinie stepped out as did the other driver.

"Phoenix."

"Henderson. Who's your passenger?" Agent Phoenix inquired.

"Jerrod Weldun, *Hothead*." Agent Henderson motioned to the back of the cruiser.

"He still at it, huh?"

"Yeah. Apparently he was reformed and then relapsed; next

thing you know, buildings are torched."

"How'd you put him out this time?"

"Chased him through the park. Threw a low grade explosive into the sandbox. Doused him." Henderson explained.

"Good plan."

"Uh, guys..." Agent Martinie pointed to the back of the cruiser where smoke drifted from atop the window.

"Looks like things are heating up, Henderson." Phoenix motioned.

Agent Henderson's view joined theirs and sighed with an eye roll. Phoenix's lips pursed as if he wanted to laugh. Martinie waited to see what this inferno of a man in custody was going to do. Henderson turned and leaned into the driver's door.

"Oxygen extraction." He said.

"Cleansing now." The mechanized voice of the car's computer said.

The three agents waited and watched as the cruiser whirred and the smoke soon cleared up. The man in the backseat fell unconscious.

"Well, I better get him logged in. Agents." He gave a nod and got in.

Phoenix and Martinie continued on their trek.

"So, Hothead?"

"Let's call it a chemical imbalance. To put it simply, he sweats fuel. If cars still ran on gasoline, he'd be a rich man."

"Do they reform often?" Martinie asked.

"It's rare. But it gives me an idea."

He looked at the street sign and drove another two blocks before taking a left and then a right at the next street. The block appeared run down with warehouses and garages on either side. Rusted machine parts lay outside the long-shut large doors. Phoenix parked outside a brown and gray building, an about-face to most of Carbine City. He pointed to a set of stairs that led above the garage.

"Here we go."

"Where is *here*?"

"One of the reformed... I hope."

When they reached the top of the steps, Phoenix knocked. They stood while someone was heard moving around on the other side. A moment later the door opened and a middle-aged black man looked at the black boots up to the rest of the uniform.

"Oh shit."

"Hi, Murph." Phoenix smiled.

"I don't want any trouble, Phoenix. I'm, I'm retired, reformed, you know that." The man said with his hands up.

"Relax, I just have some questions. I thought maybe you could help us out with a familiar problem."

Murphy stopped and thought about it before backing up.

"Well, come on in."

He led them into the loft, lived-in with knickknacks and machine parts scattered about. Dishes piled in the sink and food lay on the counter. Murphy cleaned the newspapers off the couch.

"Murphy, this is Agent Martinie. Martinie, this is Murphy Elliott."

They greeted each other then they all sat down, Elliot in a ratty recliner and the agents across from him on a seldom-used couch.

"Before reforming, Murphy here was the king of thieves."

"I was the best." Murphy said with a chuckle that led to a cough.

"Something to be proud of." Phoenix sarcastically said.

"I live a quiet life now." He motioned around his place. "So what's the problem?"

"An Agency craft was stolen from the garage. Security footage was blacked out. Have you heard or seen anything about it? Know anything?" Phoenix asked.

"I don't know jack." He shook his head.

"Have you seen any cruisers driving suspiciously or where they normally wouldn't be?" Martinie joined the questioning.

"Like I said, I don't know anything."

Agent Phoenix thought to himself for a moment.

"You used to use a technology to steal vehicles without touching them, hijacking them from a separate location. Could that be what we're looking at?"

"I don't know. Those are old school methods. Child's play compared to what runners are doing today. It's just an outdated method. It was changing when I got out of the game." Murphy explained.

"Well, then-"

"Phoenix. Come in, Agent Phoenix." His phone alerted.

"This is Phoenix."

"An Agency cruiser was just seen on the south end of town sideswiping two parked cars before speeding off."

"Roger." Phoenix turned to Martinie. "Looks like our ride is here."

They rushed out, leaving Murphy behind, thankful he was no longer involved in such action. After jumping in the cruiser, they took off.

"We got something." Martinie said of the monitor's beeping. "We're on the right course. Whoever it is, is zig-zagging all over the road."

"We gotta hurry before they hurt someone."

Agent Phoenix stepped on it and they flew forward down the street. Bike riders were too slow in getting out of the way, along with walking pedestrians. Phoenix was growing frustrated and turned on the siren, cranking up its intensity. Passersby covered their ears and ran out of the Agency craft's way as its booming bass frequency rippled through the air.

"Damn that's loud." Martinie winced.

"You think it's loud in here, try being them." He pointed out to the cowering civilians holding their ears.

When there was a clear path, the cruiser shot forward. They sped around the corner, siren still blasting. Those on the street could tell it was of great urgency and hurried along. Phoenix maneuvered with ease and controlled the rising speed.

"We're gaining on 'em." Martinie said with his eyes glued to the monitor. "Whoa, just took a sharp turn."

"Hold on!"

He jerked the wheel to the right and cut through an alley. They sped up again and burst through a stack of pallets and emerged in the next block over. The tires skid and screeched as it spun, almost hitting a delivery truck head-on. Phoenix swerved in a near miss.

"They're going around in circles..." Martinie was puzzled.

Martinie braced himself again when he saw his partner's hands grip the wheel and foot force the pedal down. They edged closer to the light on the screen but it began to flicker.

"It's, it's losing signal. We have them, then we don't." Martinie informed.

While Martinie kept him up to date, Phoenix became almost one with the cruiser as his body drove and his mind went into a deep focus. Deep within Phoenix's eyes, past the chocolate brown, and through the black, he saw ahead of him the complete layout of the city from memory. The people and objects blocking structural views were the same as in the layout, but he had to get through that stampede and try to time the social clusters, as well as predict the traffic pattern beyond the building ahead. He swerved right then left again, nearly missing scared pedestrians. Straight, to the next block, then right.

"Closer... CLOSER..." Martinie was on the edge of his seat.

The engine revved a final time as the target came in sight in the distance. Getting closer, they saw it in a parking lot doing donuts. And even closer, it was clear that the cruiser was spinning out of control. Phoenix came to a park and they both got out. The driver pulled the craft's circles in tighter.

"Stay here!" Phoenix yelled over the sound of the squealing tires.

He ran along the outside to where the spinning cruiser was directly between the two of them. Phoenix drew first, Martinie followed as both had the potential driver in sight. They looked closely, squinting, bending.

"See anybody in there!?" Phoenix asked.

Martinie was having trouble seeing much detail but he could see that no one was visible in the driver's seat; judging by his question, Phoenix had seen it as well.

"No!" He shook his head. "We should try to shoot the tank!"

"No, don't! The water spills out and this thing could hydroplane out of control!"

The stolen cruiser bucked and gyrated like a wild bronco. Phoenix looked to his partner, intermittently blocked by the mechanical mass spinning amok, and pointed down. They ducked down in unison. Agent Phoenix waited for the time to strike. A window of opportunity, Phoenix shot into its front driver's side wheel well. Martinie followed, hitting the opposite side. They fired once more as the speed of the cruiser died down with a sad whirring as it...wound...down. The whirring became an over-pressured whistle before finally dying between them. Weapons still drawn, they opened the doors. It was vacant, as they expected. Phoenix got in and tried its central computer.

"Phoenix to base from the AWOL craft. Come in, base."

Silence.

"This is Agent Phoenix. Come in."

The blank monitor pixelated and broken voices came through the frequency.

"Reading you, Phoenix."

"No driver. Can you trace its controls?"

"The signal's faint but it's showing its power source is on a rooftop...across the street."

Phoenix and Martinie got out and looked up and over. It didn't take them long to cross the street. An apartment complex was the only building across from the parking lot tall enough to hide someone on its roof. Phoenix called for cover from his partner and went in. The two walked up the stairs on high alert, their eyes shifting back and forth with their guns securely on point. Up another flight and they reached roof access. The agents looked at each other, nodded, and opened the door quietly, just a crack. They flung the door open and sprang into action. Phoenix rolled through with Martinie rushing out at his six. To their shock, under their aim were two young boys. The kids froze seeing the agents and the guns they pointed. The older of the two children held a large remote control as they both threw their hands up in fear.

"Aww man." The older boy groaned.

"He *broke* it." The younger said.

Phoenix looked at Martinie with a sigh and they holstered their firearms.

It was a long ride back to base with the children in tow.

"What were you two thinking?" Phoenix asked.

"We just wanted to have some fun and the Agency cruisers are so *cool*. Just wanted to drive one."

"Yeah, our parents never let us have any fun." The younger boy pouted.

"Yeah, well, your fun could've hurt a lot of people. You could've killed someone." Phoenix reprimanded them.

"You wanna drive an Agency craft? When you're old enough, see if the academy is interested." Martinie told them.

"That's right. There's a right way of doing things." Phoenix added. "Where did you learn that technology anyway?"

"A kid at school. He took his dad's car out. Showed me how."

"Child's play, huh?" Martinie echoed Murphy Elliot's words.

Phoenix drove and explained to the boys that it was going to be their last joyride for some time, especially once their parents learned of the damages they'd be paying for. Other agents would've had a laugh at the situation had the thought of it happening to them or their vehicle not come to them. The boys were thrilled at first with seeing the Agency base but the excitement dwindled once they were pulled in for questioning and soon their parents. Needless to say, security on the Agency garage was upgraded soon after the incident.

The Agency Roadway, a sector one would say looked like a mile-long empty lot, but without cracks and potholes. Perfectly paved and walled off, like the base itself, it was constructed without witnesses.

"Haven't you had enough driving today?" Agent Martinie asked. "First the stolen cruiser, then the lady with the bomb."

"I need to get my time logged in for the day, stay sharp." Agent Phoenix said and opened the door to the building.

They entered and were headed for the counter when Phoenix stopped and stepped aside. Martinie stopped as well.

"Hold up."

Martinie watched and waited as Phoenix stretched intensely. His bones cracked and popped, his muscles contorted.

"Whew, all right." Phoenix was charged.

They moved on to the counter and waited on other agents signing out. Martinie stirred where he stood for a brief second.

"What is it?" Phoenix asked.

"Oh, it's just that lady with the bomb... She didn't even know she had it on her." Martinie was still shaken by the thought.

"Yeah, well, you gotta watch who you let carry your groceries."

The other agents were done. They stepped up.

"Gettin' your time in, Phoenix?" The man behind the counter nodded.

"You know it, Mickey." They fist-bumped.

Mickey spun a tablet around to him.

"Just sign the logbook." He said as he'd told the agent countless times before.

"Of course." Phoenix leaned in and signed it with the weighted stylus.

Phoenix slid the tablet back and looked at Martinie before the two left. They walked past the counter and through the building. Out back was the Roadway. The line-up of Agency crafts was ripe for the picking and Phoenix could have his choice of any. Martinie walked with him as he looked them over. To the untrained eye it would look like multiples of the same model - all sharing the same slick body in red, white, and blue - but Phoenix could see something in each of them. Every machine carried its own story, its own aura, and the agent saw that aura.

"This is the one." He selected.

Phoenix got in and his partner walked alongside the vehicle until he reached the exit. Martinie stood and watched as Phoenix sped off.

TERROR IN THE SKY

VICTOR RAN, glistening with sweat. He ran for his life and breathed heavily as one hand shot up after the other. The treadmill beneath him stayed at a steady sprinting speed. Tobin ran on the treadmill to his left at the local gym, Platinum Bodies. The wall-sized screen before them was broken into four streams: the news, a talk show, sports highlights, and assorted infomercials - most for local products and businesses.

"Ready to move on?" Victor asked looking over to the equally racing Tobin.

"Let's hit it."

They stopped their machines at exactly the same time and hopped off. Tobin and Victor walked to the punching bag and strapped on their gloves.

"Gonna show me how it's done?" Victor grinned.

Tobin chuckled as Victor held the bag. Tobin threw punch after punch, keeping it lighter than average to not hurt his spotting partner. Right hand, left, right, left-left-right. Victor held on tight as Tobin punched and kicked intermittently. The strikes came harder and faster before Tobin realized this and stopped.

"Well that's one way of getting your aggression out." Victor said, stepping from behind the bag with heavy breaths.

"You're up, babe."

Tobin wiped the sweat from his brow and held the bag securely.

"Just like last time." Tobin told him. "And remember to watch out with your swings, you could hurt your wrists if you're not careful."

"I got this. I *got* this."

The two had a fast laugh before Vic threw punches, sloppy compared to Tobin's but that held ferocity. While still having fun, Victor got some of his own aggression out as he punched at the bag. Tobin rooted him on.

"Get it! Get it! Harder! That's it, you got it."

Victor's speed picked up to a flurry of punches. Tobin was impressed. Vic tried for kicks but they were less successful. He snickered at himself but only briefly before returning with punches. Tobin's watch began beeping repeatedly.

"All right. All right."

Tobin checked his watch and Victor stopped in mid-punch.

"Sorry, Vic, I gotta get to work for training."

"You know, it'd be nice if we could both have the *same* day off." Victor said, taking off his gloves.

"Just gotta be patient. C'mon, let's get out of here."

They kissed and grabbed their bags and left, saying goodbye to others on the way out.

Victor was dropped off at home, where he went inside and took a shower, rubbing his wrist. Tobin drove to the Agency, where he showered and suited up. After tying his boots, he sprinted out of the locker room. He didn't want to risk the elevator so he took the stairs. It wouldn't take him long before reaching his destination.

"Phoenix. Tobin."

"You were almost late." The well-suited man pointed out.

Phoenix and the man stared at each other with intensity. Then it broke. He and Phoenix laughed.

"Come on." He said.

Phoenix's badge was scanned and he was given a keycard with a small screen.

"Wonder what I got today." He said, passing through the doors.

'Training Scenario: Apocalypse.' The screen read.

He stopped where he stood, reading the system's choice, and laughed. About six feet further in and he plugged the card into the kiosk.

'Apocalypse begins in t-minus 60 seconds.' Streamed across the screen.

Phoenix walked through the door and stretched briefly before hopping up and down a few times. The long warehouse of a room was empty and stark but would not echo. The dim lights plummeted straight down to black.

The moonlight rose, revealing the streets of Carbine City worn and in shambles. Buildings were toppled as their holograms flickered against rubble and dead vehicles. Agency crafts sat broken down alongside police cruisers, bodies lay outside in piles. Screams soared through the smoky night sky. Cries for help came from the distance. Agent Phoenix was now suited in added protective gear while holding a hefty cannon. He moved forward, staying sharp.

Working his way through the dilapidated city he caught the fractured display of the news vender, now dead beneath his table.

'Bellview Topples, Convicts Escape' read the pixelated headline.

Wild cackles and delirious incoherent chatter were getting closer. Faceless crazies sprang from the darkness. Phoenix's weapon whipped over as he fired. One by one they were gone in a flash of light when hit with the cannon's lasers. Scattering was heard. He followed the cries for help when he saw her, a little girl, lost and afraid.

"Please help me. I'm scared. They took mommy."

He approached her.

"You're safe now. Come with me."

She stayed close as he searched for more survivors in need. The laughing, faceless evil lunged at the agent from behind mounds of former buildings. He turned and fired, never letting them touch him. The little girl stayed behind him, ever scared. The flashing of the beings reduced to a pinpoint of light, their manic voices faded with rippling reverb.

"We're over here! Help us!" Survivors coughed in the thick dust clouds.

Two women shielded their young son beneath a fallen wall. Phoenix made his way, blasting the scurrying crazies along the way. The family of three, malnourished and exhausted, were saved and joined Phoenix's growing collective. He led them through the ravaged streets, fending off the onslaught of escapees. A group of them crept up over a dead cruiser to his left. Agent Phoenix ducked down and shot the vehicle. The explosion eliminated the deranged four headed their way. His survivors stayed behind him. The ground shook in big bumps and thumps. Cars were thrown along with structural debris. Vocals bellowed, sounding like gravelly whale calls. People ran out of the darkness screaming for their lives when they saw the agent.

"Get behind me." Phoenix told them as they joined the group.

He aimed and squeezed the trigger, taking out random attackers while awaiting whatever was making such a sound to show itself. His group yelled and pointed as he spun and shot more.

"Stay close!" He ordered.

A building was knocked over, billowing dust and smoke into the night sky. The sound emitted again and the assailants scattered and ran away from the agent as well as what was coming. The smoke cleared briefly and Phoenix saw a towering monstrosity that defied description. A creature so hideous, so heinous, that the terrified survivors were lucky they could only see glimpses and shades of it through the debris. It stepped forward, smashing its large claws into the buildings in its way. It snatched up the crazies and threw them into its mouth before directing its attention to the agent and his survivors. He fired his weapon at it and moved around the vehicles to get better shots. The laser blasts angered the beast and damage was minimal. It hurled a brick wall as Phoenix ushered his group out of the way. He led them to a clearing.

"Stay here. I'll be back."

He ran out firing at the thing as well as the frenzied escaped convicts. The creature picked up a car and launched it at the agent who leapt out of the way. He tried shooting its legs but couldn't make out how many there were through the thick air. Its head and hungry gullet was in view so he used his scope to get a clearer shot but the blasts were doing very little. It called out again, the sound shaking what was left of fallen establishments.

Phoenix knew that he had to change it up but he also needed to get closer.

"Help me!" A man cried behind the wall of chaos.

He ran out coughing and fanning the dust in his face. Phoenix saw the man backed by the monster and ran up to help him. The man distorted and contorted to something else entirely before attacking the agent.

"Damn it!" He was tricked as the man jumped at him.

Phoenix caught him and threw him to the side before shooting him. Like the others, the man dissipated in a flash. The monster roared again, stepping forward with large quaking stomps. To Phoenix's right was a fire escape leading up a building of shaky structure. He had to take the chance and ran to it. Cars were stomped on as he climbed. He got to the top and still wasn't close enough. He fired his weapon without aim or direction to get its attention. Its eyes, more than a pair, gazed over. Phoenix pulled an explosive from his belt and waited. It got closer...closer... He activated the bomb and hurled it with all his might. The creature's jaws snapped shut, swallowing the device. The building beneath him started to crumble as Phoenix jumped down the fire escape. The bomb went off and the beast exploded, showering the streets in rays of light.

Agent Phoenix climbed down to check his survivors, shooting nearing crazies. Screeches came from the dark skies. What else would he have to battle? The group stayed close together as the agent led them out ready for what was next.

The training scenario lasted another three hours before being interrupted by a call. The air became still, and heavy. The crazed cackling had ceased. Survivor by attacker by fire by smoke by corpse, it all vanished. He looked down as his weapon and gear flickered and faded. He left the training room to take the urgent call when he was informed that the Carbine City police station was under attack.

"Agents respond. Repeat, agents respond."

Victor watched the news as footage streamed of a trio of small zeppelins circling above the station. Vic turned it up and leaned in with a listening ear.

They'd swoop down in turns blasting at the building. Police ran outside firing at it, but it was no use as they were shot down by the airborne assailants. Skybound snipers surrounded the CCPD in giant balloons with cabs where the solo pilot (and shooter) operated such a vessel. Inside, police pulled their fallen brethren from where they were shot down and fled from the windows. Cops suited up in bulletproof vests and returned to the window. They fired but it appeared the flying vehicles were armored.

The news circulated to Bellview and caused a stir amongst its inmates. Baxter watched as the others got riled up. He heard murmurs of a riot. He wasn't sure whether or not the others had the stones but still enjoyed the sentiment, and waited.

The ships flying overhead continued to rain bullets down upon the station. Agents Phoenix and Martinie arrived, followed by more.

"What the hell is this?"

The balloon-like bubbles atop the aircrafts billowed while keeping their spherical shape. The rifles attached to the cabs were stocked with ammo and it wasn't being used sparingly. Shell casings rained down on the streets below as they gunned the police station.

Agent Martinie drew his weapon but Phoenix stopped him before he fired.

"If we shoot them down, we risk them falling on civilians."

People swarmed the street in a panic trying to get to safety.

"Try to clear a way, I'm gonna aim for the cabs." Phoenix told him.

Martinie ran to the crowd and tried to usher them out of the way. Other agents joined him. Phoenix drew his gun and aimed for the body of one of the flyers. He fired but the shot was reflected.

"Damn things are armored."

The barrage of bullets continued with the gunmen unscathed. The police fired back with every shot ricocheting. A squad car pulled up beside Phoenix's cruiser and the officer stepped out.

"Was pulling in a perp when the call came through." He told Phoenix.

His eyes wouldn't leave the airships nor would those of the petty thief cuffed in the backseat.

"Get back!" Agent Phoenix pulled him out of the way as a spray of gunfire hit the squad car.

"Why would you all help *us*?"

"We fight for the same cause."

The shooting stopped.

"Release Desmond Pike!" One of the shooters called from a megaphone.

"Who the hell is Desmond Pike?" Phoenix asked.

"Eco-terrorist we picked up about a week ago." The officer answered, still unable to look away from the terror in the sky.

"Release Pike now and this ends!" Another shooter said before unloading on the building once more.

"No, this ends now."

Agent Phoenix moved to his cruiser and pulled out a rifle, powered with the same energy blasts as the Agency pistols. The policeman watched as Phoenix attached a scope and propped the weapon up on the roof of the car. He kicked himself for not thinking of it sooner. Phoenix aimed with a sniper's gun in his sights. The casings fell to the ground with metallic rattling. Phoenix fired. Direct hit. The gun was destroyed by the blast. The pilot quickly turned the ship around. Agent Phoenix saw that the way beneath them was clear and swiftly returned his sight to the small tank on the back of the ship and fired again. The airship sputtered and fell slowly from the sky. It landed in a near crash. The others turned their aim to Phoenix as other agents rushed to the fallen pilot. The agent leapt out of the line of fire. Martinie returned.

"Everyone's out of the area."

"Good. Shoot 'em down. Aim for the back. There's a tank or *something* back there."

The two dodged the oncoming gunfire.

"How do we get to it now?" Martinie asked.

"I'll draw them out."

Agent Phoenix handed Martinie the rifle and jumped in his cruiser and took off down the now empty street. The pilots turned and started to give chase. The bulletproof exterior of the Agency craft proved useful as the cruiser took the hits. One shot, two shot, and the two sputtered out of the sky. Martinie ran to the men with the weapon pointed.

"Freeze!"

Police came from the station. Phoenix got out of the car. The three men were apprehended.

"Agents, thank you." The police chief shook Phoenix's hand.

The balloons on the three ships deflated as agents and officers alike inspected the vehicles. Solo pods, armored and armed.

"Not every day you get to save the police." Martinie said.

"Hey, you never know, we may need them to help us one day." Phoenix replied.

The situation calmed and arrests were made. It would take some time before the station could be repaired to its original state.

BREAKOUT

BAXTER COMBS had been watching everyone and everything since he'd arrived. The pattern of the guards, the step count, the topics of chatter among both staff and inmates, and the bathroom habits of those around him; every little thing, he kept his eye on. When the guards had left and their conversations had become too quiet to make out, he studied the other inmates. Some caught the peering eyes and quickly looked away, while others returned the stare but only briefly. 'Not after Jethro Muldoon,' they thought.

Baxter played coy, quiet. When guards passed by he showed no signs of his violent nature. A subdued prisoner, once he was placed in a cell alone that is. It was almost time for a solo guard walkthrough. The pair had just passed through two hours prior. Combs grabbed the dingy, stained cup from his sink and waited. He counted distant steps. They were getting closer, just around the corner. He threw the cup out into the hall and crouched down. The guard turned the corner and started down the hall and, in time, came across the metal cup and Baxter Combs almost on his knees reaching out for it, straining and grunting.

"Aww big man drop his cup?" The guard said, drenched with sarcasm.

He picked up the cup and slowly stepped to Combs with

something he deemed witty on the tip of his tongue. Before he could even think to defend himself, Baxter reached out and crushed the guard's larynx and slammed his head into the cell door. In one smooth motion, he pulled him in and swiped his keycard, opening the cell. Baxter pulled him inside and shut the cell. As he started to undress the guard, he felt eyes on him. He looked around at his excited, panicked, and otherwise curious neighbors and shot them the look of daggers, and soon a sick grin. Combs finished undressing the guard and stripped down. First he donned his disguise before dressing the new inmate. He picked the man up and placed him in his bunk and covered him up. Baxter's hat was on straight, his jacket just so, and the keycard was in hand. When he left the cell, he kept his head down and his ears open. He listened for those familiar steps while remembering guard talks of having go to the Acquisitions Room to log in items; and he recounted the time it took.

His keeping track of the guards' time and steps paid off as he avoided face-to-face contact along with having to speak. Baxter arrived at the Acquisitions Room and swiped the badge. Walking through the large room he saw a set of mechanical arms, a big remote controller, and past a pulsating case of green and yellow was his cannon. His soul-stealing machine was still intact, though the barrel was dented shut from where Phoenix had blasted it. It was much too bulky to leave with it in hand so he took it apart in four pieces and concealed them in different places on him. But something else caught his eye on the shelves.

Baxter Combs walked through to the next wing, keeping his head down and nodding when addressed. William Lannerman sat in his cell still fuming that the woman who'd had a hand in ruining his mother's life walked around free. Baxter approached the cell.

"I-I don't want any trouble. I'm not doing anything." Lannerman said, seeing the guard.

"Shh..." Baxter said with a finger to his lips. "You're coming with me."

He opened the cell and cuffed the Mailman and pushed him out and led him down the hall.

"Transferring prisoner." He'd explain if stopped.

His timing was perfect. Mass's guards were on break and the beast was subdued. Baxter opened the cell and stepped inside. Lannerman watched, confused, as Baxter slapped the sleeping man in the face. Still out, no reaction. He shook him and slapped him again. Mass woke in a rage and instantly began to grow.

"Yeeesss." Combs smiled.

He left the cell. Mass grew and stomped out of his cage. Chaos ensued. He smashed into neighboring cells and walls. Guards flooded the hall. Mass picked two up and clashed their heads together in a bloody mess before throwing them into the growing crowd. While they fought to control the giant, Combs and Lannerman were gone.

Lannerman pleaded with the guard to tell him where he was being taken. Combs ignored him and kept pushing forward. Once they were far enough away from Bellview, Baxter revealed himself to Lannerman.

"What do you want with me?" William asked.

Baxter removed from his pocket the Final Notice deactivated explosive and held it up to him.

"First we hit your place." Baxter said, uncuffing him.

"I'm sure the agents confiscated my things." Lannerman explained.

"I'm sure you'll think of something." Combs held up the cuff rod in a taunt.

"I'll make it work." Lannerman nodded.

"All right, let's move."

Agent Phoenix sat in his office looking over an open folder of reports while on the phone.

"No. The prison wants Desmond Pike transferred to Bellview after this afternoon's excitement. I'm reading his file right now. They're processing the pilots as we speak. I'm not so certain I want them all kept in the same place. Might be best to leave Pike where he is and put his boys in Bellview. Well, I still gotta go through their files; I'll call again in a bit to see where we're at. Bye."

He hung up the phone and continued learning about the eco-terrorist and his cohorts.

Bellview was put on lockdown after the large inmate was found out of his cell. Guards flew into the wall with a *crack*, and a *thud* as they hit the floor. Mass was growing by the minute, hurling trained guards around as if they were ragdolls. He'd already broken a few tranquilizer guns, snapping them in two like a pencil, but the staff scrambled to get more. He bellowed a primal scream and threw an arm out, clearing the space around him of any personnel. Security tried to get a hold on him but they were no match for his strength. In an instant, Mass was painted with red dots, the laser sights of security posted up on the floor above them. They tried to get a clear shot but the beast of a man was flailing and staff kept ending up in the way. Finally, an opening in the chaos. Tranq darts rained down upon him, breaking through his tough exterior and it wasn't long before the roaring had ceased. He stopped where he stood and his eyes glazed over as his large frame began to wobble. Staff moved out of the way as he came tumbling down. Mass shrunk down in size before their eyes. They managed to keep him sedated while they repaired and reinforced his cell.

Baxter and William made it to William's place. They were watchful of their surroundings as they slipped past the Agency's black tape covering the door bearing "Carbine City Agency - Do Not Cross." Upon entering, Baxter looked for the bedroom.

"Where are you going?" Lannerman asked, while inspecting his home.

"A change of clothes. Something a little less obvious."

William nodded and searched. It didn't take Combs long to change while Lannerman put things into a large bag. Baxter stepped out and rolled up his sleeves.

"A bit much in the length and a little snug but it'll do until we get there."

"And where are we going?"

"My place. What's this?"

"They took most of my gear but I still have what I need." William said, zipping up the bag.

"Took the meal but left the ingredients. Thought you were smarter than this, Tobin." Baxter thought aloud.

Combs eyed the man's home while Lannerman picked the bag up.

"Good to go."

"Let's move before we're spotted."

They grabbed their gear and left discreetly.

"All right, Combs, time to eat." The guard approached his cell to find it empty. "What the..."

The prisoners to either side looked at the guard shaking their heads.

Agents Phoenix and Martinie responded to a call. A woman

slid a cylindrical bar into a small sphere the size of a volleyball. She looked down from the water tower she stood on and released the sphere as it floated out in the air.

"Mother Nature's a bitch." She grinned.

The mechanical ball emitted a whirring and soon the air beneath it began to turn, forming a small tornado. Cars were thrown off the road. The pointing, the staring, and the panic weren't foreign actions to the citizens of Carbine City. Despite the clear sky, the powerful micro-storm brewed. People were pulled around by the growing wind currents but that was just the start. Thunder rumbled loudly from the mechanism before electric lashes whipped out. The synthetic lightning struck buildings and vehicles. Sparks flew while some took shelter, trapped by the sudden storm. The Agency cruiser pulled up and the agents ejected from it.

"This is crazy!" Agent Martinie yelled.

"It's coming from up there!" Agent Phoenix pointed to the sphere, barely visible above the mess.

They both drew their weapons and shot at it but the tornado's power sucked up the blasts. They separated and tried again from different angles but ended with the same results. Through the gusts of wind and lightning strikes Phoenix spotted the woman standing on the water tower.

"Hey!" He got Martinie's attention and pointed her out to him.

"Something tells me she's not a jumper."

"Let's try to get these people out of here, then we'll deal with her."

They ran in but were cut off by a blunt electric strike to the ground before them, cracking it. Agent Phoenix sharply surveyed the scene. Between the force of air and the lapping lightning, there was no way of getting everyone in the area to safety without addressing the nucleus of the problem first. Parents shielded their children and held on tight in the growing winds. The agents tried shooting once more to no avail.

"Pistols are a no-go! We gotta stop that thing!"

Agent Phoenix pulled an explosive from his belt. Fitting perfectly in the palm of his hand, his thumb pressed the button on top and he threw it up. The tornado sucked it up and the bomb detonated. The explosion disrupted the air flow but only briefly.

"It's not working!" Martinie yelled.

"But we're on the right track!"

They ran back to the cruiser.

"What's the plan?" Martinie asked.

He followed Phoenix back to the trunk. It was opened revealing an arsenal of choices. Phoenix grabbed a case of the explosives and set them all.

"Once this goes off, start firing up dead center."

Martinie gave a curt nod and the two rushed in to the eye of the powerful micro-storm.

"Get ready!"

Agent Phoenix weathered the storm and planted his feet the best he could. He released the case and the spiral sucked it up. Phoenix dodged flying debris and lightning strikes. Detonation. The explosives went off in unison, forcing a momentary bubble in the storm, a clearing to which the mechanism was seen clearly. Agent Martinie fired at it and Agent Phoenix drew his pistol and joined him. Their window was short and their trigger fingers made use of the time. Shot after shot they blasted at the sphere. Just as the storm started to pick back up the machine shattered. The wind and lightning came to an abrupt halt as the pieces fell. The agents shielded citizens from the metal shards.

Martinie checked the people.

With her attack foiled, the woman came down the ladder in a hurry. When she reached the bottom she was set to race off when Phoenix snatched her by her arm.

"Hold up."

In one smooth and swift motion, he cuffed her. She stayed silent and grit her teeth beneath the hair cascading over her face. Agent Phoenix walked the assailant back to the cruiser when Martinie approached.

"Everyone safe?" Phoenix asked.

"They're good. Vehicles took most of the damage. She give you any trouble?"

"No."

Phoenix put the weather woman in the back of the Agency craft as the radio called in.

"Come in, Agent Phoenix."

He leaned in through the window and flipped the switch.

"Phoenix." He answered.

"Phoenix! Baxter's escaped!"

His eyes widened. His partner saw the look on his face.

"We gotta go."

The agents wasted no time jumping in and speeding off.

"Where to?"

"I've got to get to Victor. You take her in and get her processed."

"Roger."

The cruiser flew down the road as Agent Phoenix thought the worst.

The unidentified woman in the backseat smirked beneath her hair at the sight of the agent's frenzy. Carbine City University was up ahead. He gripped the wheel and spun the car to the curb, ejecting out near the door. Phoenix entered to a few raised eyebrows. Checking his watch, he thought hard to remember Victor's schedule in his current state. He took a chance on memory and raced down the hall.

Agent Martinie had jumped over to the driver's seat and took the lady in. After getting her to processing, he searched for Bellview security footage.

Phoenix rushed in. Victor gasped and the class sat in confusion.

"Victor, we gotta go. Now."

"What is the meaning of this?" A university staff member stormed in after the agent.

"Tobin..."

Phoenix turned to the man.

"This is Agency business. Find someone to fill in, I'm taking him with me."

They left the building and went to the parking lot.

"Babe, you're scaring me."

"Just get in, I'll explain on the way." Tobin told him getting behind the wheel of Victor's car.

Baxter Combs and William Lannerman walked through an empty field in their new clothes, passing off as average citizens who *didn't* just escape from Bellview. William was still nervous while Baxter was determined.

"So, you live out here? No wonder they can't find you."

"Not exactly. I don't really have what you'd call a permanent residence." Baxter glanced back at him and kept walking.

"How many times have you been to Bellview?"

"Conserve your energy. Askin' too damn many questions.

We're almost there anyway."

Tobin and Victor carried their conversation into the house.

"I gotta go back to the office. I want you to lock this place down after I leave and keep it locked until I come back." Tobin told him, closing the door behind them.

"Are you sure this isn't too much?"

"Vic, trust me, this guy's a psychopath. We can't be too careful."

He opened the door and closed it when a thought struck him.

"Shh, wait. Hear anything?"

Victor froze where he stood and shook his head. Tobin pulled his pistol.

"Wait here."

Victor watched as his husband moved room to room, closets to cabinets, securing the house.

"Okay," he returned, "We're clear."

Victor stepped up and threw his arms around Tobin.

"Be careful," they kissed, "And don't be gone long. You can't freak me out and then leave."

"I promise I won't be long."

From the window an Agency craft was seen pulling up out front.

"Well my babysitter's here."

"I'm taking the car. I'll be back."

A deteriorated building stood covered in vines and foliage. Lannerman wasn't too impressed. Baxter moved a loose vine and knocked on the door three times. A heavy lock was heard unlatching and Combs entered with William staying close behind. Baxter's goons sprang for their weapons at the sight of the extra man.

"Relax, he's with me."

Guns and knives were set down. Everyone was nervous as Baxter's eyes scanned the room. He took out the end piece of the life-draining cannon and threw it to a man.

"Barrel needs repaired."

"On it." The man scurried off to a makeshift shop with the piece.

Lannerman looked around as well. Shabby furniture and dingy building structure was offset by mounds of stacked cash. He noticed the table behind him holding roughly a dozen vials of the neon milky liquid.

"What's all this?" William asked.

"Rejects. Still hoping to turn a profit on them. Let's go."

Combs led the man to a back room, looking like another shop of sorts with tools and electrical equipment. Combs cleaned off a chair while Lannerman set his bag down.

"What exactly am I doing here?"

"I heard about the envelopes. I'm intrigued."

"You want me to make those again?"

"Not quite."

"Then what am I..."

Baxter took off his shirt, revealing the metallic tattoos streaked throughout his body.

The holographic security footage was pulled up. Phoenix stood beside agents Martinie and Brick as they played it, slowing it down on various parts. Baxter's escape played out before them, from the toss of a cup to releasing a monster. The exterior security footage caught their exit but only briefly.

"Who in the hell is supposed to be watching this feed?" Agent Phoenix asked.

"Guy said he went on break and his filler was working." Agent Brick said.

"So, where's the filler?"

"Home sick, he claims. Says he didn't see anything. Want to bring him in for questioning?" Brick asked.

Phoenix thought it over watching the hologram.

"No," he groaned, "Not the first time some intern slacked off. Don't bring him back."

Baxter unleashed Mass from his cage again on repeat viewing and the chaos that ensued. Phoenix shut it off.

"But what does he want with Lannerman?"

SECTOR 9

TOBIN AWOKE, his exhausted eyes struggling to blink, and quickly learned he couldn't move his mouth. He was strapped to the bed and gagged. His head jerked over to see Victor bound as well. Terrified, tears streamed down Victor's face and into his ears. Tobin's anger rose while his heart broke watching the love of his life scream muffled cries. He pulled his arms and kicked his legs but it did no good.

"Well look at the happy couple. I have a feeling this isn't how you normally sleep."

Victor shook and Tobin tried to lunge forward. Wide watery eyes from both had an image burning into their minds - Baxter Combs stood at the foot of the bed with his hands on his hips and a salivating smile on his face.

"I finally got you, Tobin. Hubby doesn't look to be having a good time." Baxter said, in love with the moment.

Victor shut his eyes tightly in hopes it would all disappear.

"I'm in a bit of quandary. If I kill *you*, then we can finally end this...whole thing. No more going back and forth. No longer having to ride the brink of insanity. No more nightmares."

Tobin struggled as Baxter stepped closer to Victor.

"On the other hand, if I kill your *man*, then I've won this game of ours."

He returned to pacing.

"But who do I pick?"

Tobin's eyes hit the life-stealing machine.

"Oh no, this won't be used. This will." Combs held up the agent's pistol. "You really shouldn't leave this on your nightstand. Now...back to business."

He pointed the weapon back and forth between the two bound men. Tobin worked his mouth and screamed with all his might. His body strained as he belted out and the gag came loose. Baxter looked to be settled on Victor. He aimed.

"No! Pick me! Take me!" Tobin cried out.

The gun went off and Tobin woke in a frenzy.

"No! Take me! Take me!"

He found he wasn't bound at all. Another night, another nightmare. The bed was vacant. Victor being gone didn't help the dream. He left the room to see Victor standing in the kitchen. He watched from the window, nursing his cup of coffee.

"Been up long?" Tobin asked, when he wanted to tell Vic that he scared the hell out of him.

"Got up a couple of hours ago. Couldn't sleep." Victor said before taking a sip.

"You should've woken me up."

"No. You need your rest."

Tobin stepped closer to see what Victor was looking at - the Agency cruiser parked outside.

"You okay, Vic?" Tobin worried.

"How long do I have to stay cooped up like this, Tobin? It's been three days."

"Just until we know it's safe. We've been on the hunt, something will turn up."

"How do we know he didn't leave the city? Why would he stick around?"

"Just call it a hunch."

"All right. That's it." Lannerman said making the finishing touches.

"I'm all done?" Baxter asked.

"You're fully operational."

Beyond the room to which has been worked in for three days, Baxter's thugs sat around a large table with drinks and an ongoing card game. The door to the back room opened and Baxter stepped out with Lannerman coming behind him. His band of thieves stopped what they were doing and looked up. Baxter stood shirtless with his metal tattoos wired with cybernetics, blinking and shining under the lights. His goons didn't know what to say or what to make of what they were seeing. The grin of accomplishment crawled across Baxter's face.

"Boys, we just changed the game."

Mouths and cards dropped.

"I still don't understand what the point of this is. You're a walking bomb."

"Your job here is done, Mr. Lannerman. Your services are no longer required."

Baxter held a hand out as one of his men placed a handgun in it.

"But wait, I can – I just –" Combs shot him where he stood.

"Take him out back and leave him for the wolves."

The surveillance hologram ignited and the office had eyes on the collage. Carbine City streets and businesses were seen in crystal clarity.

"No sign of him yet, sir." The worker told Agent Phoenix.

"What's the game plan?" Agent Martinie asked.

"Well, first we take care of that in Sector 9." Phoenix leaned forward and maximized the noted sector.

Two mechanical hounds terrorized a group of civilians. They shielded themselves from the snapping metal jaws.

"Let's go."

They jumped in. Doors slammed shut. Belts fastened. The key turned. Acceleration. The Agency craft sped down the busy streets en route to the ninth sector where cyber-beasts were wreaking havoc. The crowd of people screamed and cried at the lunging of said beasts. One man pulled his kid out of the way and kicked at one of the mech-mutts when it bit his leg, taking it clean off. Their steel jowls snapped and chomped with metal clanging. The citizens couldn't take their eyes off them. They came up about waist high with spring systems visible in their legs. Their claws were sharp screws at the end of blunt paws. A mechanized snarl emitted from them and the lights in their eyes glowed red.

In the distance, well-beyond the hounds, stood a man waving

his cyber gauntlets like a symphony orchestra conductor.

"Possessions. Now!" A mechanized voice came from one of the beasts.

Confused and terrified, the people looked to each other and back at the machines when the next hound gave the same command. They scrambled to remove any worthy possessions. One of their four-legged assailants sat and leaned its head back. Its jaw unhinged and its mouth opened wide and a large hose emerged. Shakily, civilians started dropping rings, watches, wallets, and more down the metal gullet while the other continued to snap and snarl.

They cried and dropped more before the hose retracted and jaws returned to their ferocity. The other sat and did the same and everyone followed suit. Within the crowd, a man leaned down to pick up a loose brick. He pushed through those in front of him and hurled the brick with angered exclamation. It hit one of the beasts in the head, knocking it back. The other was still in retrieval mode. It shook its head and leapt at the man. The crowd spread out in screams as it took the man to the ground.

Shots rang out, blasting off the mutt's head before it could bite down into the man's face. The other retracted its hose and stood alert. Agent Phoenix and Agent Martinie ran into the melee but were cut off by the snapping metal jaws of the mechanical terrors. They wanted to check the crowd for their safety but one glimpse at the legless man holding his bloody stump gave them their answer. The agents squared off with the hounds. They fired again but the shots did little damage to their chrome exteriors.

The beasts jumped at and snapped at the men who shot at them. The shots merely kept them back. They wanted to kick them back but quickly thought against it. The crowd exclaimed while watching the agents take on these things; some fled the scene while others stayed and stood frozen. Agents Phoenix and Martinie jumped back, evading attacks, and swung their pistols at them when not shooting. That's when Martinie noticed the man beyond the crowd. His eyes scanned the man up and down, noticing his eyeing them and the crowd, along with the machines on his arms.

"Phoenix!" Martinie pointed out the man.

The agents shot and swatted at the jumping dogs as Phoenix looked over to the man in question.

"You got this?" Phoenix asked his partner.

Martinie looked at the two snarling machines before looking back to Phoenix with uncertainty but ultimately gave a curt nod and tried to distract them. Martinie moved to one direction as the remaining crowd backed up. The man turned to run as Phoenix gave chase. Martinie found the previously-used brick and kicked it up at them while firing his pistol.

"Halt! Freeze!" Phoenix shouted in his sprint.

The man did not comply and ran.

Phoenix stopped, aimed, and fired a blast at the man's feet causing him to tumble forward to the sidewalk. With one hand he reached forward and pressed a button on the opposite gauntlet. One of the terror machines snapped at Martinie and got a hold of his sleeve. He shook the beast around but his jaws were clenched shut tight. Phoenix made it to the man before he could stand and slammed his knee down into his back.

"Gotcha."

The man began to laugh manically. Martinie kept his hanger-on busy, shaking him about, while shooting at the other. The man continued to laugh as Phoenix pulled his arms back to cuff him.

"Something funny to you?" The agent asked the apprehended man.

The cuffs barely fit around the gauntlets.

"I just took the leash off." He cackled.

Phoenix noticed the blinking light and turned back to the man's mechanical dogs. The one hopped off of Martinie's arm and stopped beside the other. The two shook and shivered. Martinie stood confused. The snarling escalated as the two appeared more feral than they had seemed previously. Phoenix pushed the button next to the blinking light but there was no change.

"Once they're off, they're off." The man laughed.

The beasts lashed out at everyone around them, more ferocious than before. They were quick, wild, and fierce. People panicked and Martinie shot at the fiends. Phoenix tried pushing different buttons on the gauntlets only to see no change. The controller of such monsters continued to laugh at the agent. Agent Phoenix picked him up and walked him back to the area.

"What? What are you doing?"

"We're gonna see how loyal they are." Phoenix told him as he pulled him along.

If it was included in their design, the mutts would've been foaming. They spun and jerked around with almost rabid movements as they jumped and snapped wildly. The closer the agent and the perp got, the more nervous the man was becoming, and his laughter had subsided.

"No. No!"

Phoenix brought him into the commotion. The mechanical dogs turned to see the approaching men and snarled. Phoenix held the struggling man forward. He cringed and shook. One of the beasts leapt with open jaws but Phoenix stuck his pistol in its mouth and fired. It fell back and gyrated and whirred before *exploding*. The contents which were inserted into its gullet erupted into the air as jewelry and wallets rained down. The man breathed a sigh of relief.

"Martinie, aim for the mouth!" Phoenix instructed.

"Hey! Hey, over here!" Martinie yelled shooting at the other.

He got its attention as it turned, chomping its jaws at the agent. He shot but couldn't match the blasts up with the jaws and they kept reflecting off of its head. Martinie sucked it up and stepped forward, plunging the end of the weapon into its mouth in mid-bite, and fired. Sparks flew and it whirred before it exploded as well. The civilians were relieved as they watched their belongings fall to the ground. The two beasts lay in smoking piles of machine parts. Their legs twitched slightly, making people unsure about rushing to collect their things. When the kicking had stopped and the smoke was cleared, everyone went in to get their stolen items. Martinie exhaled and holstered his pistol.

"You're going away for a long time." Phoenix told the man who groaned.

"I'll call the medics and cleanup crew."

"Good. Call them then we'll take him in."

The agents entered Phoenix's office.

"That was close. At least it's over." Martinie stated, sitting down.

"Yeah, but we're still no closer to finding Baxter."

"We'll find him, Phoenix."

"I'm gonna go home real quick and check on Victor and then we can get back to searching."

"Where will we be looking? He could be anywhere."

"Then we'll search the darkest parts of this city. I'll be back. Keep an eye on things." Phoenix left.

Victor heard the door and a sudden panic set in as he jumped up from the couch. Tobin entered and Vic was relieved.

"Hey, babe. Just came by to check on you and see how you

were doing. Make sure you were safe." Tobin said.

"I'm fine." They kissed. "Just don't like being cooped up. It's making me paranoid. What if we got a dog?"

"No." Tobin said sharply. "Don't even mention dogs. You'll be fine. We're about to go look for him now. I just wanted to make sure you were okay."

"Just a prisoner in my own home, but safe considering."

"You still have an agent looking out for you outside. If anything happens or you get a strange phone call, let him know immediately."

"I will. Be careful out there."

"Hey, you know me."

"Exactly." Victor smirked.

"Yeah, yeah."

Tobin kissed him and left. Victor watched from the window as Tobin stopped to talk with the watchful agent. What they discussed, he couldn't make out but he assumed it was about him and the situation.

Agent Phoenix returned to headquarters where he left with Agent Martinie to go on the hunt for Baxter Combs. They searched and searched, showing a hologram of Baxter to anyone they could, but the trail went dead after hours. Victor grew more nervous when he heard the results of the search but Tobin assured him that he was safe.

Meanwhile Baxter Combs sat in an undisclosed location, one of the many hiding places he'd found. His crew counted stacks of cash while he eyed a table of full vials thinking to himself. He thought of Tobin and Victor and looked down at his newly acquired cybernetics.

"Soon, Tobin..."

New Addition

"HONEY, I know you're feeling locked up but I have to go out tonight."

It was evening when Agent Phoenix arrived to the scene: a break-in at a storage unit. Phoenix got out and looked down the long row of sheds. Agent Martinie joined him.

"Looks like the only one opened." Martinie said.

"That's what I'm seeing."

Phoenix walked up to the opening, stopped, and looked down.

"Acid..." he said, nudging the nasty spot on the corroded concrete.

"They really wanted in there."

"Yeah, let's check it out."

Phoenix pulled his flashlight and stepped inside, Martinie followed suit. What the light didn't hit was black. They searched the darkness.

"Ah!" Martinie jumped back.

"What?" Phoenix spun around urgently.

"Nothing. Just a damn cat." The orange cat passed them and left.

Looking around, seeing the best they could, it was hard to

figure out what they were looking for. Boxes and loose items strewn about.

"Just looks like junk. Why the B&E?"

"Must not have found what they were looking for. Or maybe-wait, shh... You hear that?"

They froze and listened. Something was barely audible deep in the dark silence. A repeating hum. Phoenix followed it. The beams of their flashlights crossed and eventually fell in together as they got closer. Their lights landed on a pile, neatly stacked compared to the rest of the shed. They started taking the pile down carefully as the pulsing hum was becoming clearer. A folded dusty old blanket and a cracked mirror were moved and the previous hum became a sharp beeping. In a topless box was a bomb with a timer at 7... 6... 5...

The agents scrambled through the clutter and dove out of the unit as it exploded. Flames licked their heels before they landed, the residual heat still whipping at them.

"We gotta call this in," Phoenix coughed, "And get to the bottom of this."

Baxter's henchmen piled into the room. He and another were looking over his device.

"Van's gassed up, boss."

"Bags and vials are ready."

"Good, good." Baxter looked around him, grabbed a couple of stacks of cash from the pile beside him, and threw it to his soldiers. They snatched at the money like wild animals and roadkill.

Meanwhile the man sitting at the table stared at Baxter with a smirk.

"It's easy, isn't it?" He motioned to the other two, now happily counting.

"You're still here, aren't you?"

He shut up.

"All right, boys, listen up. I've got the list, but first... we're gonna make a quick stop." He powered up his machine as his men flinched. Deep down in the barrel a blue glow grew brighter.

Victor looked at the Agency cruiser still parked outside. His protector was in his usual spot. After a while of watching the house, he'd get out and search the perimeter, like clockwork. Victor pulled his attention away from between the blinds when his phone rang.

"Hey, babe." Victor answered seeing Tobin's name.

"Ah, I'm sorry, Vic, it's gonna be a late one for me. I don't know what time we'll be able to wrap this up."

"Okay, I understand." Victor groaned and blew it off. "I'll see you when you get home."

"I love you. I know you're cooped up now but it won't last forever."

"I hope you're right." Victor glanced out at the agent again. "Be safe. I love you."

After ending the conversation he changed his mind about cooking dinner and decided on popcorn instead. With the kernels in the popper, he waited. As the popping began so did a knocking at the door. It gave Victor a jump. He looked at the door questionably as the knocking continued.

"Needing a refill on your coffee?" Victor asked on the way to the door.

They knocked again.

"I'm coming. I'm coming. Probably need to use the bathroom after all that time out there."

Victor opened the door. His heart jumped and any expression dropped. Baxter Combs stood in the doorway looking this man over.

"You must be Victor..."

Victor froze as Baxter entered. He was intimidated by the stocky figure outlined in lit circuits. His men followed in behind. Baxter walked forward. Victor stepped back. Combs eyed the home of his rival.

"You have a lovely home, Victor."

He walked in further. Victor watched him carefully while shaken.

"You probably hadn't heard of me before all this. No, I doubt he ever talked about me."

"What do you want?" Vic's fidgeting hands became fists.

Baxter quickly soured and stepped up to him.

"I wanna put him through the same hell he puts me through. I want him to have to live knowing I beat him."

"You'll never beat him." His fists tightened.

"Of course you're gonna say that. You're his pretty-boy." Baxter scoffed.

"Pretty-boy!?"

Victor threw a right cross, then a left hook. Combs took the hits and came back with one of his own, clipping Vic's jaw. He fell back and shook it off before throwing himself on Baxter. In a fury of blows, Victor rained down with haphazard swings, soon becoming full Gatling-style slaps. Baxter's boys looked at each other and fought hard to not laugh. They had watched as Baxter stole countless lives and turned a hefty profit; they had seen him kill one of his own; the boys had seen a lot with Baxter Combs but they'd never seen him get slapped around like this. Their attention was sobered when Baxter grabbed Victor's shirt amidst the fury, reared back and knocked him out. All sound seemed to have ceased with the contact of the punch. Victor dropped to the floor, a crumpled mess, and his crew straightened up. Baxter snapped and waved, reddening and growing angrier by the second. They handed him the device and he kicked Victor.

"Hey! Wake up. I want you to *feel* this."

Baxter thrust his arm into the machine and activated it. Its electric hum in the air. The boys came in to raise him up. That hum, once distant, was now growing louder and definitely closer as Victor woke up to the barrel of the cannon pressed against the back of his head.

Another explosion threw flames about in reckless lashes. Agents Phoenix and Martinie ducked down. More explosives were hurled in the junkyard with fiery results. The heat waves coming through were peeling the exteriors off of vehicles. One in particular's engine *popped* and *burst* due to the intensity of the heat. The agents braced themselves and activated the coolers in their uniforms. A breath of relief.

"Damn it!" Phoenix yelled, while attempting to fan his face.

"Well you wanted to find him."

Phoenix shot him a look. They were surrounded by piles of plastic parts and dead motors. Bombs were going off, radiating heat and melting the piles. The smoke billowed to the night sky. Agent Phoenix looked up through the flames and saw the explosives chucked through the air. Another hit. This one closer, louder.

"Move. Move."

The agents rushed to another large pile consisting of half a car, plastic and fiberglass, its engine removed. The two ducked down. They still couldn't see the man they'd traced to such a location. Martinie waited for Phoenix's move. Phoenix looked through the pile they currently used as a shield. Then he saw it - the detonation light on the bomb. He jumped up and shot it. An explosion of sparks revealed their perp. Phoenix motioned to Martinie to go around. Martinie nodded.

"Go."

The agents separated around the dead vehicle and ran through the junkyard keeping low. Phoenix turned the corner as a thud sounded in front of him. He looked down at the small oval canister blinking with light.

"Oh sh-"

Phoenix jumped back as the bomb went off, throwing him into a pile of junk.

"Ugh!" The fall hurt like hell and he had trouble moving at first.

Martinie went around the other side to find a man with a wheelbarrow of makeshift explosives. Phoenix climbed out of the rubble. Agent Martinie approached.

"Freeze!" His weapon aimed.

The man turned, silent and smiling, tossing a bomb up and down in his hand. Agent Phoenix made his way to them.

"Hold it right there!" Phoenix ordered.

The man turned, stuck between two agents.

"Why are you doing this?" Martinie asked.

The man silently laughed and shook his head before pressing the button. It emitted a beeping with its blinking lights.

"Drop it!" Martinie shot his hand, causing him to drop it inside the wheelbarrow.

"Martinie!" Phoenix yelled in aggravation.

All three men dove in separate directions. The resulting explosion was massive, obliterating the surroundings. The flames were limited but the damage was severe. Debris dropped and the smoke was thick. The soundscape was near silent, save for the falling particles of junk. No sign of any of them through the mess. A decimated vehicle sat.

A groaning was heard. The trunk opened and Agent Phoenix climbed out before falling to the ground, coughing and catching his breath. He tried to get himself together and stand but it was taking more effort than normal. The bomber crawled out from beneath wreckage. He pulled himself forward by his arms, dragging his legs behind him. His hands were stopped and pulled behind him before being cuffed. Agent Phoenix picked him up but the man could barely stand.

"Still nothing to say?" Phoenix asked, holding him up.

The man mouthed words but nothing vocal came out.

"Well your hands seem to be working, you can write your statement."

Phoenix stopped and looked across the wasteland.

"Martinie..." Worry set in.

There was no sign of anyone let alone his partner.

"Martinie!" He called. No answer.

He dropped his perp.

"Have a seat."

Phoenix searched the area calling Martinie's name.

"Damn it, Martinie." He sighed and feared the worst before digging through the rubble.

The silent bomber watched as the agent dug around. Phoenix coughed from the smoke and fanned the thick dust. He'd burnt his hands lifting large pieces, and shook them. Then he heard it, the coughing. He stopped, alert.

"Martinie!"

He tried to trace the sound but all he could see was chaotic piles of junk. Phoenix continued to dig. Movement some feet over. He rushed over and started hurling mechanical pieces to the side to find Agent Martinie coming to. Wearing black smudges and hacking up from smoke inhalation, Martinie's eyes blinked before seeing Agent Phoenix above him. Phoenix extended his hand to his partner.

"You really scared me, Agent."

Martinie took his hand and was pulled up to his feet. They dusted themselves off.

"Did we get him?"

Phoenix looked at him in his rough state and chuckled lightly.

"Yeah. Yeah, we got him. Let's go."

Carbine City Agency. Agents Phoenix and Martinie brought in the limping, apprehended man and delivered him. The agents were blackened and their uniforms were in shambles.

"Rough night? You guys look like hell."

"He's mute. You won't get a word out of him." Phoenix informed them.

"So, we mark him down as Silent but Deadly?" The worker smirked.

"Don't write that." Phoenix turned to his partner. "Get a shower and some rest. I'll be in my office."

Martinie left, still clearing his lungs. Others were brought in with their captors looking to have a cleaner night. Phoenix entered his office and sluggishly removed his jacket. A groan let out from his tight shoulders. He collapsed in his chair with an exhausted sigh. He saw the clock and new Victor would more than likely be in bed but he picked up the phone and dialed. It rang, and rang. *'Yeah, probably asleep,'* he thought. He rubbed his head as dust fell to his desk.

The door slung open as his head shot up.

"Phoenix, it's Victor." Agent Brick said with urgency.

His eyes grew wide and he jumped up from his seat.

Tobin, accompanied by Agent Brick, arrived home to find it marked off with tape. Agents worked.

"Why didn't anyone tell me?"

"We tried. Couldn't get through to you."

The agent on watch outside was found with a knife in his throat. Apparently his demise was so quick there was no time to react. In the house, past the tape and through the agents, Tobin made his way to Victor. His husband lay on the floor, appearing dead to the normal eye. Tobin's eyes welled up and he gasped. He dropped to the floor and lifted his lifeless love. Tears of anger flowed as he held him close.

"I'm sorry, baby. I'm so sorry." He cried, gripping him harder.

A thought hit him and he turned his head over and ran his thumb along the familiar puncture wound before crying out more.

"That son of a bitch! I'll kill him!" Fury swelled in him and was spilling out.

"We'll get him, Phoenix." Brick told him, with a hand on his shoulder.

Tobin pressed his head to Victor's and sobbed. The agents present had never seen him like that. Agent Phoenix broke down as he held the love of his life, beating himself up for not being there.

"We'll get him to base. He'll be safe and taken care of."

"No." Tobin said sharply. "Set it up here. I want him here with me."

Brick watched the agent in despair, wishing he had the words to help aid his broken heart.

"We'll get you back, Vic." Phoenix held Victor close and wouldn't let him go.

WE'RE NOT GOING ALONE

DAYS HAD passed. Tobin's five o' clock shadow had grown in nicely, and he never left Victor's side. Victor Louis-Phoenix lay in bed hooked up to monitors supplied by the Agency. Tobin sat next to him. He wanted nothing more than to track Baxter down but he didn't want to leave Vic alone. A manhunt had begun the night Agent Phoenix's husband was taken from him. No trace of Combs was found but the search continued. Tobin didn't know how he'd live with himself if Victor's consciousness wasn't returned to him. Vic made life worth living to Tobin. Their relationship is what often pushed him to be better. Now he watched him in perpetual slumber, waiting for him to wake. Tobin saw it in that time - Victor would wake up and look over to him.

"Why the long face, agent?"

Tobin would rush to his side.

"Victor!"

"Who'd you think it was?"

But that waking moment never came. Victor just slept, and Tobin watched. His pistol stayed by his side like a well-trained watchdog ready to pounce the second something jumped off. The chair he stayed in wasn't as comfortable as it had been days prior. He got up, kissed Victor's forehead, and moved on to the kitchen for something to eat or to refill his coffee. Everywhere he turned in his house he saw Baxter. Shaking it off was the first step. Convincing himself that he wasn't really there was another.

He poured a fresh cup. He thought about food for half a second but was still too sick to his stomach to eat, settling on the coffee. When he wasn't watching Victor's breathing, Tobin was watching his phone. He hadn't been to work or out of their home since that night as it wasn't the right time to leave his ailing man.

Beyond Tobin's world Carbine City didn't seem to change much; not as much as it had for the Phoenix household. Drivers pulled up to fuel stations to replenish. There was a price drop on premium distilled water, though it was expected to spike back up soon. Vendors sold and consumers purchased. CCPD were on the prowl making their quota. The Agency stayed busy bringing in the city's villains. Reconstruction was done to the downtown area after lengthy explosive battles. Workers were painted with the bright colors of holographic ads. The falling of an agent's husband didn't stop Carbine City from moving forward.

A citywide manhunt was issued for Baxter Combs. Agents were sent out in search of the dangerous criminal while the police were also given a heads up to keep a lookout while out on the beat.

Night fell and Baxter Combs had work to do.

"I'm impressed." The man said, looking at Baxter's briefcase of vials.

This was Don Fatelli, also known as Donnie Fats, a local mob boss. Overweight, as his nickname would've suggested, with thinning hair and a mechanical arm. One of its primary uses was the cannon feature, and Fatelli was known to be trigger happy. He had two nephews standing beside him as he sat behind a large round table. He considered Baxter and his deal. Baxter looked at Don and then down to the vials of people. He looked at one in particular and thought about his next move.

"I'll take 'em." Don said, reaching for them all.

Combs stepped up, stopping him and took out the one he spied.

"Hold up."

"Oh, what the hell is this?" Fatelli clunked his weaponed arm on the table.

"This one's not for sale."

The man looked at him questionably.

"Must be valuable."

"A more personal keepsake."

"I see."

He looked the open briefcase over. It contained a dozen vials of milky neon liquid, the thirteenth now in Baxter's hand. The information screamed from within. One of the nephews handed Combs his money.

"Pleasure doin' business with you." Baxter told him with a curt nod.

"If these prove lucrative then we may be doing business again."

"I'll warn you, I'm not so cheap the second time around."

"I'm sure we'll reach an understanding. By the way, how's the manhunt coming along?" Don Fatelli asked with a sly grin.

"Well, I'm still here."

"You are everywhere right now. Agents are on you somethin' fierce."

"Feel like cuttin' a new deal?" Baxter asked looking at the vial in his hand.

"A place to lay low?"

"More like taking care of a certain agent."

"Oh no." Don shook his head. "I don't mess with the Agency and the Agency don't mess with me."

Baxter chuckled and muttered under his breath, though unheard.

"Be seein' ya." Baxter Combs took his payment and left.

The manhunt was underway. Agents searched the city high and low but never found Baxter. Where he could be had the Agency puzzled. Every villain arrested was questioned if they'd had known or seen Combs. Those that *did* happen to know him, the mention of his name turned their mouths crooked. They were of no help but finally off the streets. Police records were checked, an annoyance to the force. Nothing turned up but the patience of hardworking cops. As many citizens as possible were asked if they'd seen the man shown on the holopod. Nobody had seen him and were instantly in fear of a madman on the loose. The agents suggested keeping doors and windows locked, or upgrading their security. At the base, workers sifted through hours of surveillance footage from all around Carbine City. Long days and long nights, overtime, from the office workers to the field agents. They finally had to go to the one who would probably know him best.

"We're sorry to bother you in your time of mourning, Phoenix."

"Something tells me this isn't a personal call." Tobin said, pouring cups of coffee.

Advisor Thomas sat with Agent Brick and Agent Martinie to either side of him. The three looked at each other with unease.

"Let me guess: you can't find him." Tobin said, sitting across from them.

"We need your help, Phoenix." The Advisor said. "We've searched and searched, nothing comes up."

"You know how he works. You've been on his tail for years. You know how he thinks." Martinie said.

"We gotta get this guy, Phoenix. Or else what happened to Victor is going to happen to a lot more people." Agent Brick added.

Tobin sipped his coffee and considered their request. The gentlemen drank, awaiting an answer.

"He doesn't stay in one place very long. He's a nomad, a gypsy. He packs up shop and moves on."

"So he's probably moved to places we've already checked." Martinie said.

"Exactly. Every last hideout I'd found he'd left decaying."

"What about habits? Anything or anywhere we could catch him at?" Advisor Thomas asked.

"I can't tell you how to predict his next move, he doesn't go by a code or a pattern. He's unpredictable and chaos is his only order." Tobin explained.

"We need you to come back, agent. If anyone can find him, it's you."

Tobin exhaled and stood up.

"I told you, I'm... I'm not ready yet. I need to be with him. Like I should've been. Now, if you'll excuse me."

Tobin saw them to the door.

"If I were you I'd check and double check potential buyers." He told them.

Martinie turned back and looked at his disheveled partner.

"This sulking isn't you. This isn't going to bring him back, you know."

"I know. I fear nothing can bring him back."

With that said, Tobin closed the door. He returned to the bedroom where the Agency had set Victor up. Tobin entered and looked over the hoses and cables attached to his husband and sat down in the chair beside him. He took a deep breath and buried his face in his hands.

The three left the Phoenix household and headed towards headquarters. Brick drove.

"I've never seen him like this." Martinie said. He looked out at the city going by.

"It's like this just stopped him in his tracks." Brick added.

"He's been dealt a hard blow." Advisor Thomas sighed from the backseat. "Tobin Phoenix is a decorated agent and I'm afraid he won't be back. We need him. This city needs him. Victor needs him."

"He'll be back. There's no way he lets Baxter beat him. We gotta find him." Martinie said.

"I hope you're right, agent. For all of us."

A commotion was up ahead. A cacophony of destruction. Brick tried to look around the cars ahead of them. Vehicles swerved to dodge the oncoming terror on wheels. A truck, armor-plated, and raised with massive tires. Collision. Sparks flew. The truck plowed through traffic smashing smaller vehicles and knocking others off the street. Cars and SUVs flipped and were hurled off to the side. Brick didn't see it until it was almost too late. The car in front of the agents halted abruptly with a head-on smash. Brick jerked the wheel hard in time for the backend to be rammed. The Agency vehicle spun as the truck took out the next car. Brick and Martinie jumped out.

"Stay here, Advisor Thomas." Agent Martinie said, pulling his pistol.

"I was in the field for longer than you've been alive." The older man said.

The Advisor pulled up his pant leg to retrieve the pistol from its holster. He got out and joined the agents. The truck came to a stop after getting lodged between a store van and partly on top of a taxi. Broken glass was scattered around the streets. Twisted metal in hissing hunks. People screamed. People shouted obscenities.

"Check those people out." Advisor Thomas told Martinie.

"On it, sir."

While the young agent tended to those in vehicular turmoil, Thomas and Brick approached the truck. The door flung open. Guns raised.

"Come out slowly."

The driver stepped out in a large coat and a ski mask. Pistols poised, the driver's hands went up. Advisor Thomas reached over and pulled the mask off to reveal a laughing young woman. Thomas and Brick looked at each other and then back at her. She continued to laugh at the agents as they cuffed her. Agent Martinie ran up.

"Just got a call. Big break-in at the pharmacy."

"The pharmacy?" Brick asked.

"Cleaned it out."

"And you were the decoy." Thomas said to the driver.

She laughed in his face. They took her away.

The life of misery, to such a degree, was wearing on Tobin, but he refused to leave Victor's side. He read to him. Victor's NoveLite had over a thousand downloaded novels and novellas that he was actively working on, so Tobin continued for him.

"But Charles," Tobin read, "There's something I need to tell you.

"Yes, Mary. You can tell me anything.

"The house on the lake my father gave us, it's...it's haunted.

"Uh oh, Dun dun DUUUN!" Tobin gripped Vic's arm in an attempted scare. He laughed and then cried with the reminder that he's laughing alone now. He composed himself and continued reading.

He was growing weary. His five o'clock shadow was nearing a beard. His hair was becoming shaggy. His lack of movement was making him weak. He read to Victor during the day, described a television show, and at night he stood guard, triple checking every bit of security and surveillance. His pistol had returned to its bedside position. He kept thinking about what Martinie had said.

Agents Brick and Martinie were on the hunt for the pharmaceutical thieves. Advisor Thomas took the bad driver in. A tip on the street led the agents to the whereabouts in a possible medical deal going down.

"An old garage? Really?" Brick said. "Very original."

"Looks like a possible new shipment coming in." Martinie noticed.

Their brief stakeout was coming to a close. A truck pulled up and unloaded medications.

"All right. Let's get 'em." Martinie loaded a freshly-charged clip into his pistol.

"No. Wait."

The young agent exhaled and turned to Brick questionably.

"I wanna see how many more show up before we make our move." And before Martinie's next question became audible, "See, we *could* move now and stop it, but there's a chance that the complete merchandise isn't there yet. We wait until there aren't any more drop offs. They start to close the doors then we assume they're not expecting anyone else. We move in. That's it."

"I've worked with Phoenix long enough to know that's never it."

The two chuckled before their attention was pulled to the next truck bringing in the next load as expected. Men unloaded the truck as they had previously. Another truck came soon after.

Victor lay in bed, attached to his various monitors. The beeping pulsed and ticked. Tobin kissed his forehead and checked the machines before exiting the room. He checked the perimeter of the house and poured himself a cup of coffee. He sat down at the surveillance center he'd set up and sipped his coffee while viewing the screens. He'd heard a noise from the bedroom and jumped up in an instant. Rushing into the room he found nothing had changed. Victor lay there helpless. His machines worked and whirred. Tobin checked the window, under the bed, and in the closet. Nothing.

"I think I'm hearing things, babe." Tobin rubbed his eyes and left the room, shutting the door behind him.

He returned to his surveillance and took a drink before sitting down. His eyes scanned over the screens. One flickered with snow before cutting to black. His brows furrowed and he tapped the screen. Another flickering before a solid image: Baxter stared into the camera's lens with his sickening grin. Tobin's eyes grew wide and his heart jumped. Baxter, just outside the front door, held up the vial of Victor. Tobin grabbed his pistol and ran for the door and slung it open.

Tobin woke up still sitting in the chair beside the bed. Short of breath with eyes darting back and forth, he stood up and did his real check all over again. His surveillance was as it had been: dead with no sign of Baxter. He walked over to the TV and looked through media cards beside the box before selecting one and inserting it. He thought he might as well catch up on current events since he couldn't sleep restfully.

The medicine thieves began closing the garage doors. The trucks had all left.

"All right, let's move." Brick told Martinie.

They got out and drew their weapons and slowly approached the building. Brick motioned to Martinie and crouched down before checking the door. Locked. They stepped back and shot the door open and rushed in. It was devoid of life. They moved from the office to the garage to find large quantities of stolen goods, medicine of different types.

"Looks like they've been at it a while." Agent Martinie said quietly.

Someone came around the corner. Their pistols shot up.

"Freeze!"

The man put his hands up as the agents approached him. He whistled sharply and backed up as men entered with firearms aimed.

"Drop 'em, agents." They said.

Agents Brick and Martinie, outnumbered and outgunned, looked at each other with a quick succession of thoughts going through them. A nod from Brick and they fired at them while breaking off in different directions. The expected gunfight ensued. Bullets flew from the hoods while light blasts came from the agents.

"Watch the merchandise!" One shooter yelled to another.

Large crates of medical supplies acted as barriers. The agents jumped out to fire before pulling back. They shot each other a look and motioned to where their shooters were. Brick and Martinie ran across the opening, firing at the gunned men, crossing one another to their previous places. The thieves shot back as the bullets hit the floor in a messy trail. Agent Brick pulled a device from his jacket and gave a motion of his hand to his fellow agent. Martinie checked his weapon's charge and returned the gesture. Brick threw the piece of tech up and back and it exploded into a large flash of light. The shooters hollered and both agents jumped out and took out two of them with blasts to their legs and shoulders.

There were still unseen thugs heard from the agents. Agent Martinie ran over to Brick and the two started making their way through a maze of large shipments. A man jumped between the agents. Brick's hands went up under the aim of the man's gun when Martinie put his pistol to the back of the man's head.

"Drop it."

The man obliged and his weapon came down. Brick took aim

while Martinie cuffed him.

"Where are the others?" Brick asked, pushing him forward.

"I'm not telling you anything." The man laughed.

A shot went off. They ducked back, pulling their perp back with them.

"They're over here!" He yelled, before catching an elbow to the face.

More shots followed. They backed up, pulling him along, when they found double doors and pushed them open and entered.

Tobin curled up with Victor in the bed, maneuvered around the wires and tubes. He laid his head on Victor's chest and listened to him breathe, or the machines breathing for him. He cried, thinking about never seeing his husband as the young, healthy man he was. Tobin thought of all the times he should've killed Baxter and blamed himself wholeheartedly for Vic's current state. He was tormented. His drive was gone. The once-fierce agent who struck fear into the city's villains was broken as his strength was taken from him.

Brick and Martinie entered the backroom with their cuffed man in tow. Machinery filled this space like the crates of medicine did beyond the double doors. A cluster of men stopped what they were doing and quickly took up arms, spinning around to the agents. The Agency pistols came up.

"Drop 'em!" Brick commanded.

The agents stepped in further. The crowding men separated to reveal a man in a hospital bed half-covered in cybernetics. The machine's breathing was loud.

"Agents, come in." A voice came from the man without his mouth moving.

"What in the hell is this?" Martinie thought aloud.

They approached the bed-bound man.

"You're all under arrest for the theft of medical supplies."

"As you can see, agent, I'm not fit to go anywhere." The men were getting antsy. "I have a rare disorder and I was denied the help I most desperately needed. Now, I take from Carbine City. No one shall have what they require without coming through me first."

"So you're just gonna hold medication and supplies ransom because you got a raw deal?"

The shooters from the garage ran in through the double doors.

Martinie spun around. They were now between the two groups. Brick kept his aim on the cybernetic man.

"Call them off or you go first."

The tense silence swelled. Trigger fingers were itching. Sweat beaded. The man under the gun thought about this. Brick edged closer with his pistol poised. The surrounding men gripped their guns and posted up.

"I believe you, agent." The man waved his still-human hand and his men dropped their weapons.

An exhale of relief.

"But you know we can't just let you walk out of here..." Wicked grins emerged on the faces of his henchmen.

In such a position, the agents had to dig deep into their training. Both agents reached into their belts and threw down tablets which exploded into smoke. The smoke was thick in the room as the agents went to work. Laser blasts flashed in the thick atmosphere. Punches and kicks were heard. Coughs came from the man in the bed. When the smoke cleared his eyes adjusted to find all his men incapacitated. Martinie went along cuffing the unconscious bunch while Brick approached the man.

"Don't worry, we're not going alone."

A VILLAIN'S VILLAIN

THE EVILS of Carbine City seemed to have had grown in the absence of Agent Phoenix. The prisoners of Bellview were in an uproar, many put there by the agent. The Agency was doing what it could: patrolling city streets, stakeouts, manhunts, some arrests, a few fatalities. Agents worked hard but the growing threats were proving too much for them in their current state. The recent untimely deaths of agents, including the man chosen to protect Victor Louis-Phoenix, along with their star agent taking leave, meant that the sudden villainous wave came at the worst possible time.

Tobin sat back in his chair reading Victor's NoveLite aloud. The doorbell rang and his sentence stopped. He put the reader down and grabbed his pistol from the bedside table and left to investigate.

"You stay here." He told Victor.

Tobin walked through the house, passing the surveillance setup on the way to the door. He'd already seen who it was but still had the gun in a firm grip. He opened the door.

"You already know the answer." Tobin greeted Joshua Martinie, who held up a case of beer.

"What was the question?"

Tobin sighed and smiled.

"Come on in."

Tobin led Martinie to the kitchen where they took two drinks out and put the rest in the fridge.

"So, not a work call."

"Social visit. Just a couple of guys hanging out. Figured you could use it."

They sat down in the living room and started on their drinks.

"You look like you've been having a rough go at things." Tobin said. "How's Brick liking taking my shifts?"

"He's ready for you to come back. We all are."

"I know. I just can't bring myself to leave him."

"It's not your fault, Phoenix."

"I don't think Victor would feel that way."

"It's not. You can't control Baxter. Like you said, he's a lone wolf that does what he wants."

"He's a dog that needs to be put down."

"We're searching for him. We are. I don't know if you've checked the media lately but we've been getting bombarded."

"I saw. They're coming out of the woodwork."

"It's getting bad out there. How are things with Victor?" He motioned to the next room.

"He's stable. All I can do is make sure he's safe."

"That's not all you can do and you know it."

"I go looking for Combs and he comes back to finish him off."

"He's got what he wanted, to incapacitate you. To take out the great Agent Phoenix. I've seen you take on some beastly foes but never seen one get under your skin like him. What is it with you two?"

Tobin took a drink and thought about everything Martinie was saying. The young agent awaited something that would tie it all together, the missing piece of the puzzle. Tobin debated an explanation before finally speaking.

"Back before I was an agent, before Victor, I was in a tumultuous relationship. I wanted to make the world a better place and he wanted to take that world as his own. He was a bitter young man. Always angry and never satisfied. That young man..."

"Baxter Combs." Martinie said in shock.

"Baxter and I were together for a few years. Things would get physical on occasion. It wasn't always bad but when it was, it got really bad. Despite the chaotic relationship we were drawn to each other."

"So, what happened?"

"I joined the academy and he went headfirst into a life of crime. I still loved him but it was unhealthy. We split but our paths continued to cross. At first, I'd hear about his exploits and run-ins with CCPD, always wishing he'd put his drive and anger towards something good but it just wasn't meant to be. Then things changed. He showed up with the weapon and began selling lives. I'd always hoped I could turn him around but he can't be changed. He's smart, cunning, but as feral as they come. He's deadly. I've feared the day my time with Baxter would catch up to Victor. Now that we're here, I'm at a loss."

"So, Victor never knew about Baxter?"

"No. We decided coming into this that we'd leave our pasts in the past. But mine's come back to haunt me." Tobin got up to replace their drinks.

"You're the only one who knows Baxter Combs. You're the only one who can stop him."

"It's not that easy."

"Do you still love him?"

This question gave Tobin pause.

"No. We're always drawn to each other but it's definitely no longer love."

"Tobin, you gotta—" A call came in. "Yeah? All right, I'll be there." Martinie hung up.

"Didn't think you were on the clock."

"Yeah well, we all have to be on call since the uprise. I gotta go. Take care of yourself, Phoenix. And think about what I said."

"Be careful out there, agent." They shook hands and Martinie left.

Agent Martinie made his way to headquarters to suit up and respond to the oncoming calls. Tobin thought back on his rocky relationship with Baxter and his wonderful relationship with Victor. It was as if he and Victor were slipping away while his connection to Baxter continued. The love he once felt for Combs in his younger days had become a burning hatred. He finished his drink and paced, stewing in his anger. Anger fueled by loss, by defeat. Tobin threw the bottle with a barking yell. He quickly thought of what Victor would say about such lashing out, and picked up the glass pieces.

He returned to the bedroom to the beeping and whirring of his husband's living. He sat in the bedside chair and leaned in to hold Vic's hand.

"I'm sorry I didn't tell you. I should've, I know. I just..." Tobin put his head down on Victor's hand and trailed off into unintelligible stammering about wishing to change things. "I wish I knew what was going on in that head of yours..."

Alas nothing was going on in his head. Victor lay there, a shell of a man. While his body was basically lifeless, his soul and lifeblood screamed from inside a glass vial.

That very vial hung around the neck of Baxter Combs. He retracted the next vial for sale. The body fell, a head security officer. He looked around at the other bodies lying about.

"Boss, we're running out of room for any more." One of his henchmen said closing the case.

"Then *make* room. We're just getting started."

Baxter and his crew piled into the elevator. The music played a soothing tune. The ride up took a while. Baxter waited patiently while his men looked at him and his weapon then to each other. A thought transferred through their looks, *How long before he uses that thing on us?*

The elevator came to a stop and a *ding* chimed. It opened and Baxter waited as his crew left.

"Hey! You can't be in here!" More security.

Combs stepped out and the well-suited security looked at this man lined with cybernetics and holding a large chrome cannon. They scrambled to pull their guns but were shot down by the Combs gang before they could. The target was Senator Bruce Nightingale. He heard the gunfire out in the hallway and became panicked.

"Stay here, Senator." The other two in the room with him left to investigate.

They walked quickly to the door before looking at each other, listening.

"Sounds clear."

"Yeah..." The other nodded.

One opened the door slowly and stuck his head out. Nightingale watched as the man retracted his head with a pistol held to it. The door was then *kicked* open the rest of the way as Baxter's goons entered followed by the man himself. The large office housed, along with the senator's desk, a minibar, two chairs, and a couch - all leather, of course. The two men were pushed down onto the furniture. Baxter walked in slowly and confidently, his boots louder than the scared men's murmuring. The senator froze and trembled the closer Baxter got. With the soul-stealer on his right arm, his left hand moved swiftly out. The senator jumped and yelped. Baxter grabbed a cigar from the box on his desk. Nightingale shook as Combs leaned in to retrieve the lighter.

"Have a seat. Relax." Baxter said lighting his cigar.

He turned around to address the other two, blowing smoke rings, as his crew gave him some space. Nightingale went behind his desk and sat nervously.

"And that makes you two...?"

"S-sp-speechwriters."

Baxter erupted into laughter. His men chuckled along.

"You'll bring in a pretty penny." He turned back to the senator. "But you'll bring even more."

"How much do you want?" Nightingale shivered out.

"Money. I should've seen that coming. What I can get *for* you far outweighs what I can get *from* you."

Senator Nightingale regained his composure, took a deep breath, and rubbed his eyes.

"What can I do *for* you?"

"How's your memory, Senator?"

"I have a wonderful memory."

"Do you remember phone numbers or do you just rely on your contact list?"

"What?" Nightingale's nervousness returned.

"Do you remember passwords or does someone else take care of all that?"

"Uh, I..."

"I'm starting to wonder if you're worth the time and effort."

"I don't understand." He said shakily.

"He doesn't understand. Line 'em up!" Baxter shouted and threw the cigar to the side.

The speechwriters wildly exclaimed as they were snatched up, brought to their knees. Baxter walked over powering up his machine.

"No, wait!" Nightingale yelled out.

Too late, the first writer hit the floor. Baxter tossed the vial and it was caught and placed with the others. The senator shook as did the second man. Baxter placed the barrel to the back of his head and squeezed. Nightingale couldn't take it anymore and ran for the door, caught by Baxter's men before he could make it.

"Enough of this cat-and-mouse shit."

They held the shaking man while Baxter extracted his lifeforce. Combs held up the vial and saw the possibilities. An extra man ran in.

"Boss, we gotta go! Not much time before there's responders."

"We got what we came for."

Baxter and the Combs gang left the senator and his writers to be found. With their maximum capacity for the vials of souls exceeded, Baxter was now on the lookout for possible buyers. They filled the van and left. The ride was quiet. Baxter looked down at Victor's vial around his neck and thought of Tobin in agony.

"Where does all this end?" One of the men spoke up.

The others cringed. Baxter eyed him.

"What was that?"

"You escaped from Bellview. You have all this money. You even beat Agent Phoenix. Where does it stop? When are you done?"

Baxter was shocked yet impressed by the young man's moxie.

"It ends right here and right now... for you."

The van stopped while crossing the bridge. The door opened and Baxter threw the man out and over the edge. The van continued.

"Any other questions?" The men shook their heads furiously. "Good."

The doorbell rang. Tobin left the bedroom and headed for the door, not looking at the distinguished older gentleman in the surveillance monitors.

"I already told you, Martinie..."

Tobin opened the door and his heart jumped.

"Director Wachowski." He stood stunned.

"Tobin Phoenix. Pleased to finally meet you."

After uncharacteristically stammering, he let Salvatore Wachowski into his home.

"Can I get you something to drink?"

"No, thank you. That won't be necessary. Have a seat, Tobin."

They sat in the living room opposite each other. Tobin was astonished that he was sitting down with his hero. Salvatore Wachowski was around Tobin's height, of medium build, in a suit, with gray hair and an equally gray mustache.

"What brings you by, sir?"

"Sal, please."

"I have so many questions."

"I'm sure you do. Tobin, I've been briefed on your situation and I want to give you my condolences. How is your husband?"

"He's safe. I'm with him now..." His words fell silent.

"Like you should've been then? Yeah, I know. It's the price we pay for being Agents. We fight to make the city, the world safer but we can't always be present."

"Yeah." Tobin nodded.

"I've been divorced twice over my chosen profession. I lost my last wife to cancer. I was with her for her final days but was absent for most of the marriage. When she got sick, I stepped away from the fieldwork. When she was gone, I became accustomed to a life of solitude. Oh, how I miss it..."

"It's never too late, you know."

"It is for me, agent. But I understand your walking away. I wouldn't have missed the time I had with her during her fight for anything. Be there for him, protect him, love him, but get back out there and fight for him. There's a time to grieve and a time to fight."

Tobin took in what Director Wachowski was saying.

"This Baxter Combs has really stung you, but he didn't kill you. It might feel like it but he hasn't." Wachowski thought to himself for a brief moment while Tobin seethed at the thought of Baxter. "You know, I had my own Baxter Combs."

"Lenny Letcher." Tobin had read all their storied battles.

"That's right. Eh, he was a nasty man. A villain's villain. Went by his own code. No one in the Agency knew him like I did. I knew how he operated. Was usually able to call his next move. He'd always find a way to make it personal. Threatening my family, sending messages, leaving crime scenes specifically for me to see. It got bad for a while. But that's what this life is. We're put here to counterbalance guys like that. You're the flip-side to Combs and you may be the only one to stop him. The other agents are talented hard workers but you're the one with the connection and you're the one with the stakes, and those stakes are high."

The men looked at each other in knowing silence and Tobin thought about his time off and how he was no closer to getting Victor back to his old self.

"Well, I won't keep you." The director stated as he stood. "Agent Phoenix."

"Director." The two shook hands.

"Keep fighting the good fight and remember, you're the one."

"Yes sir." Tobin nodded.

Tobin walked him to the door and Salvatore Wachowski left, escorted by agents to his car. Tobin was still in shock and awe. He only wished Victor could have met him. He watched the official Agency car leave and went back into the house. Victor lay in bed with his monitors beeping and whirring. Tobin watched him with voices and thoughts whirling around in his mind. His anger towards Baxter grew.

"You haven't won..." Tobin said through a clenched jaw as his fists tightened.

BACK IN THE SADDLE

THE VOICES of Wachowski and Martinie as well as his own inner voice overlapped and echoed through Tobin's head. He sat bedside looking at Victor.

"I know what I have to do. I'm sorry, Vic, but I gotta go to work for a while."

He stepped into the bathroom mirror and lathered up his scruffy face with shaving gel and commenced shaving. His hair had become shaggy. There was no time for a cut so he'd just slick it back out of his eyes when he got out of the shower. He made his calls to the Agency, stunned to hear from him. He was dressed and ready, as ready as he'd ever be, he figured. Tobin took one last look at Victor with a heart of conflicting emotions.

"I'm doing this for us. We'll get you back, get you whole again."

He stopped himself before saying anything further. He bent down and kissed Victor's lips and left. Upon opening the front door, two agents arrived to keep watch and to monitor Victor.

"Agents." Tobin greeted them.

"Don't worry, Phoenix, we'll take good care of him."

The agents went inside as Agent Phoenix left.

Pulling up into the Agency parking garage he had a strange combination of feelings: one that had him feeling like it'd been years and the other, another day at the office. He entered the locker room to cheers and enthusiastic greetings from others changing clothes. He humbly greeted them in return before opening his locker. The picture of he and Vic gave him a brief pause, then the fire within him roared.

Tobin stretched to sore dormant muscles and cracking bones. Others in the gym watched the agent's return. First, he worked his cardio, running on the treadmill. His legs were tired but he pushed through. He ran as if he could see a fully functional Victor in the distance. Tobin was working up a good sweat before jumping off to hit the weights. A little pump, nothing too strenuous. His muscles glistened with sweat and he grunted with each lift. The agent hit multiple stations before even thinking of stopping. He was fired up and feeling good. It was time for the bag.

Tobin approached the reinforced combat bag and strapped on his gloves. He took a moment, closed his eyes, and regulated his breathing. When he opened his eyes, the bag had become Baxter. His fists clenched tightly and his teeth grit. Kicks and punches were unloaded on the bag. Blows of fury. Others in the vicinity stopped working out and crowded to watch Phoenix deliver combinations of attacks. One more solid punch and the bag came off its chain. The growing crowd reacted and the agent snapped out of it. He looked around.

"All right. Show's over."

They dispersed and he moved to the treadmill for a cool down. When he was finished, he hit the showers.

The Agency Roadway. Agent Phoenix arrived to the shock of the workers as it had happened in the locker room.

"Phoenix, you're back." Mickey said.

"Yeah."

"I'm really sorry to hear about Victor, man."

"Thanks. I got your card." Phoenix nodded. "Got a car for me?"

"Of course. Sign here."

Pleasantries and signatures out of the way, Phoenix made his way to the back. He found the vehicle that cried out to be pushed to its limit and got in and did just that. Agent Phoenix drove like he was chasing perps on the mean streets of Carbine City. Sharp turns. Bursts of straightaway speeds ending in a drift before peeling out and going again, faster, harder. As good as it felt to be behind the wheel of an Agency craft again, he had to move on. Just one more lap...

It was time for a refresher course as he settled into the training module. It had been a while since he'd run the program. The room transformed as the black and chrome walls gave way to the night-draped city. Set on an expert level difficulty, he walked forward into the alley. He was ready for whatever came at him. Agent Phoenix drew his pistol and his eyes scanned the alley on the way to the parking lot. Steam drifted up from the vents. He came upon the parking lot, full of cars.

The door to the building to the back of the lot opened and a group of coworkers came out. They talked and laughed amongst themselves, not paying the approaching agent any attention. They came out to their cars and stopped, looking forward in his direction. A quick squint and their eyes adjusted in the darkness before growing wide. They pointed past Phoenix and screamed. He whipped around to find three shadowy figures, agile and inky black. Two climbed along the walls to either side while the third walked down the alley. They were coming in fast. Swiftly, Agent Phoenix shot at the two on the walls and kicked high at the one coming up on him, knocking it back. The two jumped, escaping the shots tearing up the brick walls. They collided in midair and fused, becoming one.

The people behind him continued to scream and scrambled to get back in the building. The two shadow figures approached and *leapt* at him. He jump kicked while firing, making contact with both. Phoenix threw a punch and they retaliated with slashing at him. He stuck out his arm to take one out but they rushed him, wrapping themselves around his gun. They tried to force it from him but he kept a tight grip. He kicked and punched back at the things. Close quarters, a knee and an elbow and Phoenix was able to make the shot. One of the two blew apart into shadowy wisps as the other grabbed the dumpster and picked it up above its head and got ready to launch it at the agent. Agent Phoenix shot twice, one blast in each of its legs, and the dumpster came down crushing the being.

The concerned crowd peeked their heads out of the door. Agent Phoenix turned around. Ninjas dropped down from the rooftops above. The people quickly retracted their heads and shut the door. There were four ninjas, black-clad and twirling their swords. The agent scanned the four and shot at each of them. One by one, following the quick blasts, they reflected the shots with their swords. They circled him slowly, waiting to pounce. Phoenix saw Victor beyond this obstacle. He was healthy and lively and they were together again. But first, he had to get through this. Agent Phoenix cracked his neck and took a breath.

He shot at one while kicking at one behind him. Their blades swiped down as Phoenix leaned back, evading the cut. He punched and kicked while dodging the fast swordsmen. The agent took kicks and chops from the ninjas but recovered the best he could, coming back with strikes of his own. Phoenix fired his pistol. As the shot ricocheted off of a steel blade, it hit the killer beside him. The ninja disappeared in a flash of light. The three remaining moved in tighter.

To his front left, one lunged with his sword and he grabbed it and continued its follow through, stabbing one behind him about to bring down the killing blow. A flash of light and it was gone.

"Ah! Dammit!" He was slashed across his back.

Phoenix spun back, smashing it in the face with the butt of his pistol, and ducked down narrowly escaping beheading. One swiped low, one went for the head. Agent Phoenix jumped and spun sideways in between the two blades. He landed on his feet and dropped down to the ground, firing up. Another flash. Just one more to go.

The two squared off. Phoenix felt how much the time off had slowed him down but he was finding his footing. Swipe. Slash. The agent backed up. The ninja stabbed his sword forward and Phoenix jumped and flipped over him and the ninja kicked behind him, sending Agent Phoenix into a parked car. He turned and fired rapidly as the dark assailant swung and reflected each shot. Phoenix kicked at him and fired once more, knocking the sword from his hand. He saw a window and grabbed the ninja and stuck the pistol under him and fired. Flash. Gone. He caught his breath, awaiting the next hurdle.

The people came out terrified but relieved that the agent has disposed of their could-be attackers. Loud blasts tore into the wall and the cars in the lot.

"Get back inside!" The agent commanded.

They followed that order and fell over one another in a rush to get back inside. Agent Phoenix jumped over the first car and ducked down. He checked the charge on his pistol. He had plenty of juice. Under the car he could see many pairs of boots walking toward him.

He could hear their taunting words as well as their weapons charging up for another spray of blasts. Phoenix hopped up to his feet and jumped over and behind the next vehicle as the one he'd just left was hit and exploded. The gunmen laughed and continued to shoot. Agent Phoenix was under fire.

Meanwhile, as Phoenix was in training, Agent Brick and Martinie were also under fire. Fireballs rained from a rooftop. The agents had cleared the street of any pedestrians. Another agent was on site with a megaphone.

"Just tell us what you want! Surrender now and you won't be harmed!"

More fireballs came down, about the size of melons. They smashed into vehicles and buildings alike. When they made contact, they exploded, spreading the flames.

"He's like most of them; he just wants chaos and destruction." Brick told Martinie.

They could only get glimpses of the man with the cannon on the roof but couldn't get a clear shot. The man in question spoke.

"I wanna burn down this crooked city and everyone in it!" The man shouted down, before firing another.

"Shit, we gotta get up there." Martinie said.

"He's got the entryway blocked off." Brick replied.

"What do we do, wait for him to run out?"

"Ugh," Brick grunted in frustration. "Phoenix needs to come back to work."

The man stepped to the ledge again. Brick and Martinie took their shots to no avail. If Agent Phoenix was there, he'd try to quiet everyone down momentarily to hear the clicking in the fire thrower's tanks. They presently couldn't hear through the screaming, the mayhem. Every miniature explosion caused great damage accompanied by screams. The agents took shifts in who runs to help survivors while the other kept the criminal under watch and aim. Agent Martinie was on point and Agent Brick was out, dodging flames and tending to those cries.

"We're clear." Came through the radio. "Everybody's shook up pretty bad and there's property damage, but no one's hurt. I'm gonna try to get some of these flames put out."

"Roger that." Martinie answered.

He tried to get better vantage points, avoiding flames himself. Regardless of where he moved, he could not catch a good glimpse.

Neighbors were helping Agent Brick put fires out, bringing out blankets and water.

Agent Phoenix was down to only two of the gunmen; he'd counted seven so far. He was running out of shielding as it took a blast with enough charge to decimate a vehicle. He thought fast to what his next move would be. The agent heard the cannon's charge and jumped up to move. The blast, loud and powerful. He darted out of the way as the car exploded. The force of the explosion sent him airborne. He spun and fired, tagging one of the two who then vanished.

The last man tried to take the shot he felt he had open, but when he aimed his cannon Agent Phoenix rushed him. He grabbed and pulled on the weapon while slugging the man. Phoenix's attacker fought back. The agent knocked the blaster free from the man's hands and threw it to the side. He secured the man under the aim of his pistol. Phoenix's finger was on the trigger when a loud grumbling was heard by both men. They looked back as the steaming grate popped up into the air and Mona, the slimy gelatinous beast, emerged. She seemed larger than previous modes of training.

It slithered in lumbering motion. The gunless gunman grabbed Phoenix and tried to throw him into the gullet of the approaching creature. They struggled, grappling with each other as Mona came closer. They were too close to throw punches with much follow through, and Phoenix couldn't get a shot off. The man gripped the agent's uniform and pushed him closer to the slug-like thing. Agent Phoenix saw Mona almost upon them when he kneed him, pushed him back, and spin-kicked him into Mona, whose slithery tongue-like appendage wrapped around the man. He was dragged in screaming, slowly.

Now Phoenix had to figure out his next move while Mona was digesting the gunman. He looked for the man's cannon but it vanished soon after hitting the ground. The last man of this round was gone and the gargantuan slug had turned its attention to the agent. He swallowed and checked his surroundings for anything that could be of use. All the cars were destroyed and all that was left was the rubble of charred parts.

The beast slithered closer. Agent Phoenix opened fire and the entry wounds splatted but there was no exiting. A few more rounds and Phoenix knew the pistol was pointless, even in keeping it back so he could think. After holstering his weapon, he turned to pick up a blackened car door and launched it at the creature. Caught in its mouth, it began to crumple under pressure.

"Here, kitty!" A child's voice was heard. "Where'd you go, kitty?"

Mona shook and shivered as her body broke down the door. Phoenix looked past the feeding to see a little girl wandering through the alley. She came to the lot, saw the large monstrosity, and let out a shrill scream. The large slug swayed and turned its attention to the child. Phoenix couldn't see a way around Mona and had to think fast.

"Mona, old girl, we're gonna have to cut this short."

Agent Phoenix sprinted and ran up the large slug's body, his boots splatting in the orange gelatinous exterior. The beast reared its head back as Phoenix ran up and jumped over, narrowly escaping being swallowed up. He landed, picked the girl up, and left the alley. Mona began to give chase when it pixelated and faded. The girl also disappeared before the agent's surroundings followed. He looked up to the control center.

"All clear, agent. Good job."

'Don't worry, Vic, I'll get you back.' Tobin thought.

Fire rained down on the city. Agent Martinie returned from checking survivors. Brick was dodging flaming attacks and trying to get a clear shot at his target.

"Just evacuated two buildings." Martinie informed him.

"Any casualties?"

"No. Got some injuries, but everyone's alive. They're getting checked out now."

"Good. Air team should be here any minute."

Carbine City firefighters put out flames and rescued upstairs survivors. Agents cleared the streets of civilians. Fireballs crushed vendors' stations. Agents Brick and Martinie looked out at the blocks surrounding the building. The Agency bomb division was called as they tried to gain access to the rooftop from the building.

"Here they come now."

A black helicopter with Carbine City Agency printed on its side flew in.

"You on the roof. Stop what you're doing and put your hands up!" Came from the helicopter.

"Go to hell!" The man yelled.

Two fireballs soared from the rooftop and hit the helicopter, resulting in a fiery explosion and it came crashing down to the streets below. Damage to city property was severe and all aboard were killed instantly. No pedestrians were hurt by the crash due to the clearing. Agents rushed to the crash site. Smoke billowed and beyond the audible destruction a cackling was heard. Brick and Martinie looked up as the man stepped to the ledge.

"What's the matter, agents, can't stand the heat!?" He yelled down.

Brick tried to take the shot but the man had already retreated back.

"Damn it!"

The bomb division arrived.

"What the hell is going on here?" They asked.

"Guy up top claims the building's rigged to go if we tried to come up. See what you can do?" Brick said.

"We're on it." And they went to the door.

"It's starting again." Martinie pointed out as more fireballs came down.

One hit the fire hydrant, erupting water into the air. Distant laughter and the *vwoomf* of the launcher were heard before the fiery spheres were hurled again. In an instant the flame throwing stopped and the laughing was also gone.

"No! No! Ahhh!" Came from above.

Brick and Martinie took their attention off of the bomb division and stepped back, looking up. Puffs of black smoke had replaced the previous fireballs and there was no sign of the man.

"Hold up." Brick told the bomb technicians.

He stepped back further to attempt a better view. Martinie joined him. They shielded their eyes from the glaring sun when a figure stepped up to the ledge.

"I got him." Agent Brick raised his pistol to aim.

"Wait!" Agent Martinie put a hand on Brick's pistol and squinted looking up. "It's... It's Phoenix!"

Agent Phoenix stood on the ledge.

"The perp is apprehended. Call a cleanup crew. We're all clear up here." Phoenix shouted down.

Brick was happy to go back to his old position after Phoenix's return. When asked how he did it, Agent Phoenix explained scaling the fire escape while the man was focused on Brick and Martinie.

Brick organized the cleanup crew and tended to weary survivors. Martinie left with Phoenix to assess the growing villainy of Carbine City. Phoenix's vehicle went down the road.

"So, you're back?" Martinie asked, curious if Phoenix would be promptly returning home to look after his husband.

"I'm back. Gotta clean this city up and nab that bastard."

"How's Victor?"

"Same. No change."

"We'll get him back."

"I know."

Phoenix turned the corner and passed street vendors as holographic advertisements reflected off of the Agency craft.

"Agents respond." Came from the radio. "There's a robbery in progress. Two women in electrically charged suits."

"We're on it." Phoenix responded. "Time to go to work."

The day went on as the two agents fought a variety of foes. Bellview was getting new additions. Agent Phoenix kept a lookout for Baxter while crossing calls off his list. One by one, the villains sporadically popping up across the city were apprehended. The day was long and the battles were hard. They finished with one call and went right to the next. Attackers and thieves armed with hi-tech weaponry as well as heightened abilities. When they were done for the day their uniforms were worn and torn and their pistol clips had all run out of juice.

They returned to base as the control hub applauded Phoenix's return to action.

"All right. That's enough. Everybody back to work."

When all arrests were made and transfers and cases filed, Agents Phoenix and Martinie head back for assessment testing. Martinie was always nervous when taking the test as he wasn't sure what would signify as a wrong answer. Throughout the questioning Phoenix answered mostly with Threes coming off his adrenaline. When they were finished, they went to the meditation room. After a day on the beat he could feel his energy return. In his meditation he saw past his much-needed showdown with Baxter to a time where Victor was back, refreshed and healthy, and held onto that.

When he was signed out, Tobin returned home to relieve the agents watching his ailing husband. One agent watched the surveillance monitors while the other stayed with Victor, switching off in shifts.

"Hey. How is he?" Tobin asked upon entering.

"He's good. The same, but he's safe." The agent answered.

"Thank you for this. You're relieved now."

"Yes sir."

The man got up and gathered his things. Tobin went to the bedroom to relieve the other. The agents left and Tobin and Victor were alone.

"You have a good day? My day was crazy." Tobin sat down on the bed beside him. "There was a high-speed chase and I almost hit a kid. Came right out in the street, I almost didn't see him. Everything's alright. I just hope I don't dream about him looking up in the headlights." He shook off the thought. "I'm gonna take a shower."

Tobin checked Victor's monitors and jumped in the shower. The water rained down on him, illuminating his soreness. When he got out, he curled up with Victor in the bed.

A LINE IN THE SAND

TWO AGENTS sat at the kitchen table in the Phoenix household playing cards.

"All right. I'll check on Victor. You check the surveillance. It's your deal when we get back."

They did just that as one checked the monitors in the makeshift security hub Tobin had set up, and the other looked in on Victor. He lay there as he had since Baxter stole his life-force. His readings looked normal with no change. The security monitors showed nothing out of the ordinary as well. They reconvened to the table as one shuffled the deck of cards.

"How'd he look?"

"The same. Monitors?"

"Clear."

"I bet Phoenix is glad to get back to work."

"Yeah, after doing this for so long, he was probably going stir crazy."

"I would."

"No joke. Deal."

The city was alive with movement. People shopping and

commuting to work. Street vendors pushing their products. Agents and police were on the lookout for Baxter Combs, who was nowhere to be found. Carbine City police officers posted wanted holograms and asked around if the man had been seen. The Agency recruited the help of the CCPD when the search went to red alert. Agents scoured the city for the foe while battling others along the way. Pedestrians were stopped on the street and showed the hologram of Combs. Upon seeing the savage man, they reacted in fright and shook their heads no.

Seymour Archer sat at the Sycamore Diner drinking coffee and dunking his toast in his egg yolk. He owned the place as he did other establishments across the city. Head of the Archer family, one of the three mob bosses in Carbine City, Archer had his goons and henchmen around him as he ate. Agents Phoenix and Martinie entered.

"Boss." A man got Archer's attention, who looked up.

The agents approached the man's booth. The men surrounding Archer stood alert.

"Seymour Archer." Phoenix greeted.

"Agent Phoenix. To what do I owe the pleasure of this visit?" Archer wiped his mouth with his napkin.

"You've no doubt heard of the manhunt for Baxter Combs."

"Doesn't ring a bell."

"I'm sure it doesn't."

The two stared at each other in a polite standoff. Martinie looked around with the same nervousness as Archer's boys were looking at Phoenix.

"I was just wondering if he's approached you with some valuable information to sell."

"I haven't seen him."

"It's a matter of grave importance that we catch him. I'm sure you'd hate to lose everything due to your involvement with him."

"I told ya, I ain't seen him."

"Well, when he comes to you, which he more than likely will, keep the Agency in mind. And remember, I'll be back." Phoenix told him.

Seymour looked at the agent and nodded.

"Agents."

With that, the agents left.

"Think he's telling the truth?" Agent Martinie asked as they exited the diner.

"He hasn't seen him. Archer has a tell and it wasn't present."

"You think Baxter's gonna come to him?"

"I'd bet on it."

They were about to get in Phoenix's cruiser when they spotted a police officer. Phoenix approached him.

"Any lead on Combs?"

"Nothing." The officer said with a slight groan. "You know, we have enough work to do without having to fix Agency problems."

"Believe me, he's all our problem."

"Well, we're looking into it."

Agent Phoenix knew the line and didn't expect much.

"Keep up the good work, officer."

Phoenix returned to the Agency craft and he and Martinie got in.

"Much help?" Martinie asked.

"About as much as expected. Let's get out of here."

Seymour Archer finished his food while thinking about what wonders Baxter Combs must have. He didn't have to deal with agents often but when he did it was usually a close call on his part.

Baxter stood in his latest hideout, counting vials while wondering what big seller he'd hit up next. He had his machine retooled and touched up as he did after every time out. It was almost time to head out...

The agents checked on Victor and checked the surveillance; no change on either end. They discussed Agent Phoenix at length while inspecting the house. While they would normally envy his skill and talent as an agent, they didn't envy the position he was currently in.

Those who hadn't had the displeasure of meeting Baxter Combs were living their average lives in the city. An old man stopped by the news vendor as the kid sold him a card. The wanted hologram displayed the image of Baxter above the stand, with the words "Wanted by the Agency" hovering above. Drivers pulled into stations to refuel, complaining about the rising cost of distilled water per gallon. While the wanted images were displayed at the pumps, most who pulled up were just thankful they'd never seen the man wanted for multiple counts of murder and theft. They knew from the hologram that he was bad news, especially if he was wanted by the Agency.

Headquarters was as busy as always. Fresh coffee was brought to the workers as they scanned through surveillance images all over Carbine City. Baxter's name on the wall was the boldest red it'd been. Agency workers called for action on certain sectors where crime was afoot. While doing their usual jobs they kept an eye out for any sign of Combs. Multiple calls came through...

Agent Phoenix drove while Martinie checked his clips – charged. A call came through the radio.

"Agents respond. Trouble at Carbine City Airport and the library on Fork Street."

"On it." Phoenix responded before looking over to his partner. "Double header. I'll drop you off at the library and I'll head to the airport."

Martinie nodded and hoped he'd be able to tackle the situation solo. Phoenix pulled a sharp turn and stepped on it, hurrying through the busy streets. They pulled up in front of the library.

"Looks peaceful out here." Martinie said, scanning the building.

"Looks can be deceiving. Stay alert. I'll be back to get you."

Agent Martinie got out and Phoenix took off, ripping through the streets to make it to the airport in time. Martinie approached the building and walked in. He entered the building slowly, unsure of what situation he was walking into. His weapon was drawn. Nobody was at the front desk. It was quiet but that was expected. Then he heard a faint whimpering. He followed the sound, going up the staircase just beyond the front desk. He moved slowly and quietly when he reached a point on the stairs to get a view. Readers and staff were on the floor, cowering and whimpering, while a man paced. He was dressed in rags and carried a large cannon, not unlike the ones found in the Agency training module.

"It was a simple request: put my book on the shelves. But you couldn't do that, could you?" The man said in an exasperated tone. "No, you couldn't. *Wouldn't*. I just wanted the exposure, but now I have to do *this*." He continued to rant and rave, most of it broken sentences resulting in more confusion for the scared people on the floor.

It was obvious to Agent Martinie that this man was a

disgruntled author who was pushed to the brink. Nobody appeared injured but he needed to act before that happened. He stepped up to the top of the stairs with his pistol poised.

"Freeze!"

The man turned and shot. Martinie jumped out of the way as the cannon's blast blew the railing to pieces. The agent quickly moved behind a bookshelf.

"You picked the wrong one, agent. Wrong guy on the wrong day." The man said, holding his weapon close.

He eyed the area of hostages and they all flinched when the barrel was pointed in their direction.

"Put the weapon down! We can talk about this!" Martinie yelled from behind the bookcase.

Martinie wondered why this wasn't a call for the local police but had to help these people. After hearing the whirring of the cannon, he ducked down as a large hole blasted through the case. Books blew out and pages rained down on Martinie.

Agent Phoenix arrived at the airport, checked his clips, and got out. He entered the airport to hear the commotion but couldn't see anything through the sea of people. He walked through the crowd to get a glimpse of what he was up against. People noticed his attire and spread out to allow him through. A woman stood in the middle of the airport with a large apparatus strapped to her with a small device in her hand. Security guards stood by with their hands out.

"Miss, put it down. Come with us." They said with shaky voices.

"Don't get any closer! I swear, I'll do it! I'll take this whole place down with me!" She yelled.

Upon closer inspection, Phoenix noticed what was strapped to her was a bomb with the detonator in her hand. It looked like luggage made of cybernetics and machinery, attached to her tightly with metal bands. She noticed the agent and faced him with the detonator out in front of her.

"No! Don't move!"

Agent Phoenix holstered his pistol and approached her, stepping lightly.

"Why are you doing this?" He asked her.

Everyone else wanted to know the same. They wanted to leave but were afraid to move as she might push the button.

"What does it matter? Everything is pointless. We could all go today and it won't matter." She answered.

"Alright, I know. Life sucks sometimes. But it can be better. You don't have to do this."

"What do you know!?" She screamed and pointed the detonator out.

"You push that button and you're going to kill a lot of people. Innocent people. Children. I can get you help."

"You think you can help me?"

"Yes. I can help you. Just let these people leave."

"Let these people go." Agent Martinie told the gunman.

"These people don't mean anything." He replied before firing another hole in the bookcase.

"Exactly, so why don't you just let them go. You've made your point. You've shown them what you can do. Now let them walk away."

"Why don't *you* walk away?"

The man turned and aimed at the nearest person. The people cringed and cried out. Agent Martinie jumped up, looking through the hole of burning books, and fired. The blast went just past the man as a warning shot. He turned and returned fire. Martinie jumped out of the way and hit the floor. He peeked out from around the bookcase and shot the man's legs.

"Agh!" He fell, dropping his cannon.

The people jumped back and Martinie ran in and tackled the man. They wrestled, both scrambling for the weapon. Martinie grabbed it, turned, and hit the man in the head, knocking him out cold. He crumpled to the floor as Martinie caught his breath.

"Thank you, agent." The people told him, while wiping their wet faces.

Agent Martinie nodded and cuffed the man. He was sure the man wouldn't be going to Bellview as a man at the end of his rope and not exactly one of a life of crime.

Agent Phoenix tried to talk to the distressed woman but she wasn't hearing it.

"C'mon, just drop it."

"And miss the opportunity to take out an agent with me?"

Her previous look of stress and anguish gave way to a sinister smile. She raised the detonator and her thumb as well. Agent Phoenix drew his pistol fast and shot her hand. She screamed out in pain as her damaged hand dropped the device. Phoenix moved in on her quickly. Her hand dangled lifeless as he cuffed her. Everyone breathed a sigh of relief, agent and people alike.

"All right, folks. It's all over. Go on about your day." He instructed them.

He took her and left the airport. As he put her in the car, he tried to talk to her about what she was attempting but she remained silent. The drive to the library was long as she sat in the backseat with a large bomb attached to her. He pulled up at the library where Martinie was waiting with his man over his shoulder unconscious. Martinie put the man in the car and got in.

"Who's he?" Phoenix asked.

"Just misunderstood with a gun. Her?"

"Same. Misunderstood, but with a bomb."

"Come in, Agent Phoenix." Came from the radio.

"Phoenix here."

"Baxter's struck again. City Hall."

"Damn. Heading there now." He looked at the two in the rearview before turning to his partner. "I'll go to City Hall. You take them in to get processed. Be careful with her, that's an explosive strapped to her."

"We're driving around with a live bomb in the car?"

"The bomb division will take it off her when you get to headquarters."

"That's comforting."

Phoenix gripped the wheel and gritted his teeth. The end was in his sights, the end of his and Baxter's long-standing rivalry. The Agency craft accelerated and shot forth leaving a steam trail behind them.

The offices of City Hall looked like other places had as of late – people lying around unconscious with small puncture wounds on the backs of their heads. Agents marked off the scene. Agent Phoenix entered while Martinie drove the two to get processed. He stepped in and saw the carnage and immediately thought of Victor. He knew what the families of these people would be going through. Before he could assess the situation, the thought that Baxter couldn't have gotten far rushed to the forefront of his mind. He ran outside and looked around.

"Damn it. He could be anywhere."

He came back in as other agents were examining the bodies.

"I want to see the surveillance footage."

"Gotcha."

One of the agents took off his gloves and found the footage Phoenix required. The hologram ignited and showed Baxter and his crew in usual positions - the people lined up on the floor with Baxter behind them with his machine. One by one he took their consciousness from them. The person on the end freaked out and got up to run when Baxter's men shot and killed him. Phoenix looked over to this body which was already being placed in a body bag. Phoenix looked over the area and all the people in dire need of help.

"This needs to stop." He muttered to himself.

While he examined the scene, he tried desperately to think of how to get to Baxter before too many more were taken. When he was finished, he instructed the others to get them to safety and to notify their families. They asked what he was going to do next but he had no answer for them. Martinie pulled up shortly after.

Agents Phoenix and Martinie arrived to headquarters where Phoenix took over the surveillance hub, skimming through countless holographic images and searching for a sign of Baxter anywhere. A thought struck him.

"We need to go to the Carbine City News Station."

"I didn't see anything there." Martinie said, looking strangely at the footage.

The TV news station was currently busy with the weather report. Agent Phoenix entered.

"I'm here on official Agency business." He told them, to which they responded with whatever he needed.

The two agents watching Victor and the Phoenix house just did their rounds when they came in the living room. They turned on the TV and flipped through channels until it was interrupted by a news report.

"Hey, it's Phoenix." They said.

Agent Phoenix sat behind the news desk, facing the camera.

Baxter Combs and his goons sat in his hideout watching a boxing match when it cut to the news report.

"Hey!" They yelled when their fight got cut off.

Baxter's eyes widened with the sight of his adversary on the screen. Televisions across the city displayed the urgent report. Agent Phoenix was live and captured the attention of Carbine City. The agents watched with curiosity while Baxter watched with a cocked eyebrow.

"What are you up to, Tobin?"

"I am Agent Phoenix with the Carbine City Agency. This message is for Baxter Combs. We've faced each other numerous times but we need to do it one more time. You have something that belongs to me. I'm drawing a line in the sand. Let's end this. Tomorrow night. You'll know where to find me." The news report ended and the regular programming resumed.

"Damn." The agents looked at each other.

Baxter's boys took their eyes away from the resuming fight and looked at Combs. He looked down at the vial around his neck and thought about what Tobin said.

Agent Phoenix returned to headquarters to peculiar looks as no agent has ever called out a villain in such a manner.

Years ago. Before Agent Phoenix. Before Baxter's soul-stealing machine. Baxter sat atop of the Tyson Tower, the tallest building in Carbine City. He watched out over the city, the busy movement and the holographic advertisements below. The night sky full of stars. Baxter was bald and he hadn't yet acquired his metallic tattoos. He was younger and an anger swelled in him as he watched the city. Tobin came through the door to the rooftop.

"I thought I'd find you here." Tobin said, walking over to him.

"Hey."

"Hey."

They kissed and Tobin joined his view of the city.

"It's a big world out there."

"Eh, we should be running this city." Baxter grunted.

"I've got some good news." Tobin told him in hopes to lift his mood.

"Yeah, and what's that?"

"I'm joining the academy. I start my training in the morning."

In an instant, Baxter soured.

"What?" Baxter stood.

"I got in. I'm gonna be an agent."

Tobin had hoped Baxter would be happy for him but all he got was a punch in the stomach. Baxter slugged him, taking Tobin's breath and sending him to his knees. Tobin coughed and looked at him with disgust.

"How could you do this to me? To us? We could have had everything. We could've run this city."

"I told you I didn't want to do it that way."

"Well this is it. I'm done. You go be a pig if you want but don't expect me to be happy about it." Baxter turned to leave.

"Baxter, wait."

"It's over, Tobin. You've made your choice."

Baxter left Tobin alone on the rooftop of the Tyson Tower.

THE FINAL SHOWDOWN

VICTOR LAY in bed when Tobin kissed his forehead. He was dressed in his uniform and ready for work. The doorbell rang.

"Gotta go, babe. I'll be back."

He greeted the two agents returning to keep watch, and went to work. He drove thinking tonight's the night. He was going to face off with Baxter one more time for the love of his life. He shoved the thought of Baxter not showing up out of his mind.

"It's gonna be a long day." He said as he accelerated.

Baxter was fired up. A challenge? He loved it. *'Finally, just you and me.'* He thought. His goons surrounded him in their hideout, looking ready to pounce.

"You sure about this, boss?" They nervously asked.

"Just do it."

They all looked at each other and then back to Baxter in the center. One lunged for Baxter with a punch but he deflected the hit and punched back. The others joined in with their own kicks and punches but Baxter was too strong and too swift for them. He dodged their attacks and fought back fiercely. He kicked one, sending him back into another. One of his boys jumped on his back and grabbed his throat. The struggle was brief until Baxter flipped him over. Two came at him at the same time. Baxter picked one up above his head and kicked the other in front of him before launching the man at his crew.

They lay a pile of broken, defeated men.

"Clean up. We'll go again in an hour." Baxter told them before leaving the room.

Agent Phoenix drove as Agent Martinie drank his coffee. Phoenix couldn't get his mind off of his upcoming showdown.

"Are you ready?" Martinie asked.

"I've been ready. I should've done this a long time ago. It's just not by the Agency code."

"How do you know he hasn't sold Victor's, er, you know? I mean, information on an agent would bring in a lot of money."

"He hasn't sold it. I know him too well. No, he's kept it. That, I'm sure of."

"Well, if he~"

"Agents respond." Said the radio. "Trouble at the Carbine City elementary school."

"We got it." Martinie responded as the craft hung a U-turn and shot forth.

Children flooded out from the school screaming for their lives. Loud crashing and banging came from inside. Adults ran out with the same screams but tried to corral the kids.

"Make sure all the children are accounted for!" One teacher yelled.

The children ran around flailing and crying. Staff members tried their best to gather them up. Inside was crazier. Students and staff barely dodged the desks hurled across the classroom. Like the ones who made it out, they ran and screamed. A little boy stood in the class throwing the objects around as if they were weightless. His face flinched with tics and he trembled with heavy vibrations. He picked up the teacher's desk and threw it against the wall. Teachers ushered the rest of the panicked children out while staff tried to calm the boy.

"It's okay... It's okay..." The principal approached slowly with his hands out.

"No! NO!"

The boy grabbed his principal by his wrists and slung him across the room. The coaches on the scene tackled the boy. They tried to hold him down and subdue him but the little one's strength was too much. He stood up, lifting the grown men off of him. They shouted and tried to keep hold but he grabbed the two men and smashed their heads together. He flinched some more before shaking his head violently and screaming.

One of the teachers grabbed the flagpole in the room and jabbed at him with it like a spear. The boy grabbed the pole and snapped it in half. While the rest of the students were taken out of the school, the staff tried to deal with the little menace having a ferocious fit. He jumped on the teacher and came down on her with fists of fury. All the adults tried to dogpile on him but he swatted them away like gnats. There was no time to question the boy's strength or his sudden aggressive attitude, there was hardly time to react.

Agents Phoenix and Martinie pulled up outside and got out.

"What's going on here?" Phoenix asked teachers surrounding students.

At once all the children started telling him all about the boy and the mayhem they witnessed. The adults couldn't get a word in and the agents couldn't hear them when they tried.

"Hold on. Everybody stop!" They fell quiet and he motioned to the nearest adult.

"We don't know what happened. He just went mad and started throwing things and attacking the other children."

Phoenix looked at Martinie.

"Are you saying a little kid is causing all this commotion?" Martinie asked.

"Yes." They nodded.

Before they could go on, the agents nodded and moved to the door. The teachers held their students close while watching them enter the building, hoping they could do something about their child run amok.

Agents Phoenix and Martinie entered and looked around.

"All this for a kid."

"It's a new one on me." Phoenix responded.

Not too long and they heard where the turmoil was coming from. As they got closer to the room, teachers ran past them hollering.

"Get out of here!"

Knowing it was a child they would be apprehending, their pistols remained holstered. They stood on either side of the doorway and peeked their heads in to see the boy crushing the globe with his bare hands before punching out the windows.

"All right! That's enough!" Phoenix said, walking in. Martinie followed.

Agent Phoenix put his hand on the boy's shoulder.

"You're done, little - *oop!*"

The boy grabbed Phoenix by the hand and threw him into the pile of desks. He landed painfully with a grunt. Martinie jumped on the boy and wrapped his arms around him.

"I got him!"

The boy spread his arms out, knocking Martinie's arms away. He turned and punched the agent in the chest, sending him across the room. Phoenix shook it off and got back in. He drew his pistol.

"Freeze!"

The boy smacked the gun from his hands and picked him up. Phoenix struggled and grabbed at the boy, gripping his arm. His fingers dug into the child's skin when it tore, revealing not blood beneath his skin but machinery. Phoenix's eyes grew wide before he was tossed aside. Martinie rushed him but he spun around and threw him into his partner.

"Ugh!" The men exclaimed together.

"He's not human. He's a machine." Phoenix told Martinie.

"What do you mean, a machine?"

The question had barely left Martinie's mouth when he was picked up by the boy. The little one spun him round and round until throwing him out of the window, yelling on the way out. He turned his attention to Agent Phoenix. The agent could see his gun lying on the floor and looked back and forth between it and the robot boy. The boy charged him when Phoenix jumped and rolled, picking up his pistol on the way. He stopped, turned, and opened fire.

The shots hit the boy but he kept coming. Phoenix continued to shoot. Skin and clothes blasted off the boy revealing his true self, an angered android. Still, he moved forward, reaching for the agent with his metal hands clamping down. Martinie popped up in the window and drew his pistol. Both agents unloaded on the robot continuously until sparks began to fly. The boy sparked until he finally exploded. Martinie ducked down and Phoenix shielded himself from the flying debris.

"All right, agent. We're done here."

Agent Martinie stood up and climbed inside.

"Go outside and try to get everyone calm. Tell 'em it's over. I'm gonna call this in." Phoenix told him while nudging the machine parts with his foot.

Agent Phoenix drove them back to headquarters as the pile of dilapidated robot parts sat in the backseat. Martinie would occasionally look back at it.

"How do you explain that?"

"Can't just yet. Gonna have the lab take a look at it."

"Makes you wonder how many more like him there are."

But Phoenix couldn't think of that at the moment, though he was undoubtedly curious.

"When we get in, I'm going to jump in a training mod to get ready for tonight. You gonna be good solo for a little bit?"

"I'll be fine." Martinie nodded.

With that, Phoenix drove on with the events that just unfolded running through Martinie's brain. When they arrived at headquarters, they delivered the android to the lab and parted ways. Phoenix went to training, selecting one that would be more hand-to-hand. Martinie went to the surveillance hub and got a look at what was currently going on in Carbine City.

Phoenix's training saw him having to fight digital presentations of his rogues' gallery. One by one he duked it out with foes he'd put away. Martinie looked over the hologram footage.

"Wait, what's that?" He pointed out and they brought it to the forefront.

A gang war in the streets. At first, he thought it an issue for the CCPD but after a closer look he saw the hi-tech weaponry they were fighting with. The police arrived only to have their car shot at and totaled.

"I'm gonna go handle this." Agent Martinie said with trepidation.

"You got this, agent?" A worker asked.

He took a breath before answering.

"Yeah, I got it." He nodded and left.

While Phoenix punched and kicked his way through a revolving door of villains, Martinie raced to the scene. He saw the smoke as he approached and parked about two blocks down from the battle. Agent Martinie got closer when stray blasts flew by. He ducked back into an alleyway to avoid fire before getting any closer. He wasn't sure if this was a turf war or what but he had to stop it before innocent lives were lost. Martinie could see one of the gangs posted up behind a line of parked cars.

"Freeze!" He yelled.

They turned and fired as he jumped behind a vehicle.

The arena which Phoenix found himself fighting in was a coliseum with the attending audience the good citizens of Carbine City. He defeated Red Talon before fighting the Feeder. One by one, they kept coming, and he kept fighting.

Baxter was also getting ready, fighting his goons and taking them on two by two. When he wasn't fighting his crew, he was doing pushups and lifting heavy objects lying around.

Martinie jumped up and fired, hitting two of the five armed men. They traded shots while intermittently dodging. He caught a shot to the arm, sending him down, where he called for backup. Phoenix was working up quite a sweat as he fought Mass. The large man threw the agent but he landed on his feet. Agent Phoenix charged him but couldn't get enough force and reflected off of Mass. He picked Phoenix up and wrapped his arms around him and squeezed. The agent grunted and punched but it was like punching a steel beam. Finally, thinking quick, Phoenix dug his thumbs into Mass's eyes. He screamed out and dropped him, before pixelating and vanishing. The next villain loaded while Phoenix held his ribs and caught his breath.

Baxter got one man in a headlock and kicked another. He picked the man up and slammed him through a table. The other two jumped on him but he wasn't to be held down, and shook them off. Martinie kept fighting the good fight despite his injury. More agents arrived on the scene. One tended to Martinie, who assured them he was fine, while the others spread out. Martinie and the agents attacked and took out the first gang but were still under fire from the other. The gang members were cuffed and escorted away.

"Find out where they got these weapons." Martinie told them as they left.

Another opponent down, Phoenix was feeling the fight when Baxter Combs materialized. He cracked his neck and his knuckles and the two charged each other. Luckily, Combs didn't speak, so he didn't get under Phoenix's skin anymore than the sight of him. The two grappled with each other and threw thunderous blows.

The real Baxter Combs was fighting his crew and, though they'd had enough, he kept pushing harder. His punches became harder, slugging his men left and right.

Martinie and the agents ducked down behind cars while blasts shot over head. Martinie motioned for some to go to one side and the others to go the opposite way. The rival gang turned their attention to Martinie firing at them from behind a vehicle.

The digital Baxter kicked Phoenix in the stomach, sending him back. Phoenix jump kicked at him, followed by coming down with an elbow.

Baxter Combs continued to fight his men, but they were petering out. They came at him with all they had but it seemed no match. He let himself be hit to feel the pain and it fueled him more.

The gang kept firing as blasts flew out wildly. There was a break in the attack when Agent Martinie whistled loudly as the agents swarmed the gang members. Martinie rushed them as the agents did. Outnumbered, they dropped their weapons and threw their arms up. Martinie and the others cuffed them and took them away.

"Check the people. Make sure there's no casualties." Martinie told the agents, hearing Phoenix in his head.

The crowd of Carbine City citizens cheered as Agent Phoenix and Baxter Combs tore into each other. Phoenix threw a right hook, turning Baxter around from the force. In an instant, Phoenix jumped on Baxter and wrapped his arms around his neck. Baxter struggled, elbowing Phoenix in his ribs. Using all his might, he snapped Baxter's neck and he fell and pixelated before vanishing. The crowd erupted and soon the training mod came to a close.

Baxter's men came at him with knives and pipes he'd given them. They were nervous about going at their boss with the weapons but he encouraged it and attacked them. They were also cautious about his current setup as a human bomb, not wanting to set him off, but he fought regardless. They swung at him with the weapons but he deflected the blows and came at them with everything he had. He made quick work of them when the last trembled with a knife in his hand.

"Uh, boss, I don't wanna –"

Before he could finish, he was knocked out cold. Baxter looked at his men having taking yet another beating. He was pumped and ready. He walked over and picked up his soul-stealing machine and held it up.

"And when I'm done with you, Tobin, I'll add another to my collection. I probably won't even sell you."

Both gangs were taken in for processing but ultimately were transferred to the Carbine City Penitentiary while the Agency confiscated their weapons. Agent Phoenix finished his post-training regimen and returned to congratulate Agent Martinie on a job well done in the field. Baxter let his men rest as he did the same.

The agents watching Victor had just checked on him again when the door opened. They quickly drew their pistols.

"Agent Phoenix, we weren't expecting you." They told him.

"At ease. Just stopped in to check on him."

They holstered their guns.

"He's doing fine."

"Nobody come by? No phone calls?" He asked.

"No. Everything's been quiet."

Tobin went in to check on his husband. He lay there as he had since the Agency had set him up. Tobin checked the monitors. His breathing was right and his heartbeat steady. Tobin sat down beside him.

"I hope you understand what I have to do tonight. It goes against what I was trained for but it's the only way I can get you back. And I *will* get you back."

He kissed him and left. He spoke briefly with the watching agents before heading back out to the grind. Agent Phoenix got in the car.

"Still good?" Martinie asked.

"I wouldn't say good, but the same. C'mon, let's go to work."

They patrolled the city for the rest of the day, assessing various dangerous situations and making arrests. The day was long but Phoenix kept his eye on the prize, never letting the upcoming night stray from the forefront of his mind.

Night fell on Carbine City. Agents Phoenix and Martinie had

the Tyson Tower evacuated to avoid the loss of innocent lives. The people working weren't too happy but considered the alternative and left. The agents stood on the roof looking out over the city.

"You think he'll show?" Martinie asked.

"He'll show." Phoenix answered, looking over the ledge.

"Want me to stick around just in case?"

"No. This is between me and him."

"I hope you know what you're doing, agent."

Agent Martinie left. Agent Phoenix stretched and waited. The stars weren't all too visible due to the lights of the city. He watched the city and the movement therein. He didn't need to wonder if Baxter would back out or not, he knew him too well. The city's holograms were bright and vibrant. Traffic was its usual down below. Everyone travelling this way and that with no thought of the fight that was about to take place far above them.

The door was heard behind him. Phoenix turned. Baxter stood in the doorway holding his soul-stealer. Looking him up and down, Phoenix noticed the new cybernetics fused to him.

"Tobin..."

"Baxter..."

Baxter walked out on the roof. Agent Phoenix took off his jacket and rolled up his sleeves. The two men kept an initial difference, circling while eyeing each other.

"Surprised you didn't bring your crew." Phoenix said.

"Oh, they're here. Downstairs waiting for me when I'm finished with you. I half expected you to set me up and have your agents swarm in on me."

"No. Just me. Just us."

"The way it used to be."

Phoenix watched as Baxter took Victor's vial from around his neck and set it down before taking off his weapon and setting it down as well.

"And there's lover boy right there. He put up a hell of a fight."

"You shouldn't have brought him into this."

Agent Phoenix put his fists up tightly as his knuckles cracked. Baxter smiled his wicked grin and put his fists up too.

"Let's end this."

Phoenix struck first with a right jab and a left hook. Baxter shook off the hits and came back with a flurry of punches before they separated. He posted up in his stocky stature. Phoenix braced his stance. Baxter rushed him and they continued. Punch after kick after knee after elbow, the two men tore into each other with no holds barred. They took hits as well as giving them.

"You fight better than your man."

Phoenix's anger grew and he kicked Baxter, sending him back, before running and jumping to come down with his elbow. Baxter grunted and gut-punched him and hit Phoenix over the head with his forearm. He gripped Phoenix in a headlock and squeezed as the agent fought for air. He tightened his legs and mustered up all his strength and picked Baxter up, slamming him down. Phoenix coughed and rubbed his neck while Baxter caught his bearings.

Phoenix walked up and kicked Baxter in the ribs. When he went to kick again, Baxter caught his foot and pushed him away. He hopped up back to his feet and the two squared off yet again. Punch, punch, kick, block, and an uppercut by Baxter sent Phoenix up and down to his back. He flipped up to his feet.

"We could've run this city together!" Baxter told him and swung again. "We didn't need the Agency!"

"You went down a path I wasn't willing to follow."

"You always were stubborn. Always the Boy Scout."

Baxter Combs leapt at Agent Phoenix and pinned him. He wrapped his hands around his throat and squeezed. Phoenix tried to fight back but the grip was tight. Both men grunted and snarled at each other as Phoenix pried Baxter's hands from around his neck.

"You were nothing more than a low rent hood." Phoenix fought to get out.

"Blow me, Tobin." Baxter said through gritted teeth.

Phoenix gripped Baxter and pulled him in for a blunt head-butt, knocking him for a loop.

"That's the only head you're getting from me."

Down in the lobby, Agent Martinie and Baxter's goons exchanged gunfire. Ducking behind a pillar, Martinie popped out to send more blasts. The Combs Gang returned fire. Martinie counted four of them. As the shots rang out, he checked his clip - low on charge. He checked his backup clip and it was fully charged and waiting to be used. Baxter's boys were spread out. They didn't use their ammo sparingly as they unloaded on the pillar. Martinie jumped, firing at them in midair, and landed behind a desk. He discharged his clip and inserted the next.

He could hear them taunting him in between shots. He listened to where the voices were coming from and jumped up and fired, taking one of them down. Martinie looked behind him and saw a large metal table surrounded by chairs. After shooting some more over the desk, he turned and ran back to the table. He jumped over it, pulling it down to duck behind it. They opened fire as shots reflected off the table.

Agent Phoenix delivered a triple kick, hitting Baxter in his leg, side, and head. Baxter kicked back and lunged to spear him. Phoenix caught him and kneed him several times before Combs punched him in the ribs and threw a haymaker. Phoenix spit blood out and jumped back in the fight. Baxter pulled a knife from his boot and swung at the agent but his quick feet sent the blade flying from his hand.

Phoenix jump-kicked Baxter. He went for another kick when Baxter caught his foot and hit him in the face with a spinning elbow. Baxter's fist shot out and Phoenix pulled his arm in and put Baxter's neck in the crook of his arm. With the other hand on his jaw, he saw the end in sight and pulled but Baxter was too strong. In an instant, he flipped Phoenix over him and stomped on him before delivering rapid fire kicks.

Agent Martinie blasted another one. These men weren't dead but subdued and he had two left. The metal table was taking on too much damage and was about to give out. Martinie rushed over behind another desk, dodging the spray of bullets. Random furniture was torn up in the wave of gunfire. Baxter's two henchmen walked out into the lobby, closer to the agent.

"Come on out, agent!"

"It's over. Your partner's probably in a vial as we speak."

Martinie hoped they were wrong. The two men split up going far to either side. He saw one in his peripheral coming around the corner and had to act fast. The agent caught the man's eye and he spun to his direction. Martinie shot him in the leg.

"Ugh!"

He grabbed at his leg when Martinie ran and tackled him to the ground. More shots rang out as he ducked down while cuffing the man. When he was finished with his hands, he cuffed his feet. The last man couldn't get a clear shot and was firing out at random.

"Don't go anywhere." Martinie got out of the line of fire.

Tobin Phoenix was in the most personal fight of his life. He knew the stakes. He knew the amount of pain he'd endure. Baxter picked him up in a constricting bear hug. Phoenix struggled before boxing Baxter's ears, so Baxter released him. He kicked Combs in the groin and punched him in the nose. Blood gushed. Baxter saw red and charged Phoenix while letting out a battle cry. The agent deflected the first few punches but was soon thrown to the ground. Baxter mounted him and hammered down with blunt force, punching Phoenix in the face repeatedly.

"You've got nothin', Tobin. I know all your tricks. Know all your moves," Baxter said, in between blows.

Phoenix flipped Baxter over him as he landed with a thud. Both men lay near-broken.

"You didn't see *that* coming."

Phoenix fought to keep conscious. Baxter stood up and kicked his former lover before walking past him. He went to his machine and picked it up, inserted his arm, and powered it up.

"I'm not too sure if this thrills me or breaks my heart. I don't even know if I'm going to sell you. I may just keep you as a trophy."

Phoenix weakly got up to his knees. Baxter put the barrel to the back of his head.

"I think we both knew it wound end this way..."

Phoenix moved his head to the side and elbowed back into Baxter's knee. Phoenix rolled over and stood. He spun and kicked the machine off of Baxter's hand. Baxter ran at him when Phoenix grabbed and flipped him over the edge of the building. Baxter held on to Phoenix's wrist with a tight grip as he dangled high above the city.

"It didn't have to be this way!" Phoenix yelled down to him.

"You did this to us! Now we end it...together!"

Baxter grabbed a switch on his chest and pulled, laughing maniacally. Sharp beeping emitted. A series of thoughts and images went through Phoenix's head in waves. Chronological snapshots of his life. He looked over his shoulder at Victor's vial laying on the rooftop, turned, and kicked Baxter in the face. His grip on Tobin's wrist released and Phoenix watched as he fell screaming. Halfway down the Tyson Tower, he detonated. The explosion was large, tearing chunks out of the surrounding buildings. Tobin pulled back.

The explosion shook the building. The henchman and the agent reacted to the sound and the quake that accompanied it. The last man looked around frantically when a pistol was pressed against his back.

"Freeze! Drop it!"

He did as instructed and dropped his gun. Agent Martinie rounded them up while Agent Phoenix caught his breath. *'It's done,'* he thought. *'It's finally over.'* Tobin heard the door and almost expected a burnt-up Baxter Combs to be coming back for more, but it was Martinie. He was shocked and delighted to see his partner alive.

"Good, agent?" Martinie asked, looking over Phoenix in his battered state.

Agent Phoenix nodded, "Yeah, I'm good."

"I'll call the cleanup crew."

Phoenix picked up Baxter's machine and handed it to Martinie. He picked up Victor's vial and looked at it.

"Let's go home."

Calls came in about an explosion heard and seen in the air. No innocent lives were lost as a result of the human bomb. Baxter was gone. The agents left the Tyson Tower and took Baxter's men in for processing. Martinie drove as Phoenix watched Carbine City go past him. He felt free for the first time in a long time. He had hoped his nightmares would now subside. The hologram ads painted the Agency craft in its passing. The city was colorful at night and Phoenix was starting to see more of that color now that Baxter would no longer be an issue for him. The thought of seeing Victor again brought tears to his eyes.

Agent Martinie returned to headquarters with the last of the Combs gang. Tobin waited on pins and needles as Agency workers re-implanted Victor's consciousness. His legs jumped and hands fidgeted as he sat in the bedside chair. Tobin's face buried into his hands as he hoped and prayed that it worked, and that his husband would be back to his old self. Victor's eyes opened and adjusted.

"Agent Phoenix..." The workers said, getting Tobin's attention.

Tobin looked up as Victor peered around the room.

"Babe..." Tobin sat up and held Victor's hand.

"Tobin, what's going on?"

"You're back. You're safe."

Tobin kissed Victor's hand as tears of joy and relief streamed down the agent's face. Victor sat up weakly.

"Take it easy. It's gonna take some time." Tobin told him.

"Wha-what happened?"

"It's a long story."

Victor looked over the mess of his husband.

"Your face." Victor touched Tobin's battered face.

"It's fine." He assured him.

"Baxter, is he…?" Victor worried.

"He's gone. We don't have to worry about him anymore."

"Agent Phoenix, you've got a call." Another agent said peeking his head into the room.

"Be right back. Just relax."

Tobin left the room where a video call was waiting for him.

"Phoenix, I just wanted to tell you congratulations on your victory." Director Wachowski said. "How is Victor?"

"Thank you, sir. He'll be just fine."

"Now that you're back to work and Baxter Combs is no longer around, what's your next move?"

Tobin didn't take long to think about it.

"Actually, we're going on vacation."

Carbine City moved on without a hitch. The Agency cleanup crew had begun work on the mess Baxter left. While most of the city slept, some were still out and about. At headquarters, workers watched the surveillance hub, sifting through hologram footage of the night. Baxter Combs's name was removed from the board. Agent Martinie called it a night and went home to his wife. Tobin and Victor were together again and Tobin vowed to make sure they would never part.

Next time on AGENT PHOENIX...

THE FRONT door opened as Tobin and Victor entered with luggage, still dressed for a snowy mountain getaway. The suitcases were set down.

"As nice as that was, it feels good to be home." Vic said, kicking his shoes off.

"I agree." Tobin did the same. "It's gonna be hard to go back to work."

"I'm sure you'll manage. I can't wait to get back to my students."

"I gotta check in." Tobin said.

The two separated as Victor checked their messages. While the overhead read off calls from random people, he debated turning on the media to see what's going on in the world since their short vacation and ultimately decided against it. To Victor's delight, some of the messages were students checking on his wellbeing. He'd become the talk of the university; the teacher who had been through the horrible attack. Other voicemails included friends calling for them to call and tell them all about their trip, and a few from Agent Martinie requesting help, his voice awkward and timid. The last was a reminder that his first day back was *tomorrow*, bright and early. Victor smiled and sighed. The upside to the experience was the extra time with Tobin

Not the vacation Vic wanted, being stalked, beaten, and

incapacitated; having to go through a period of recovery including mental and physical therapy. Tobin was there to take him to his appointments. Tobin returned, his attitude different.

"Babe, I'm sorry but I gotta go. Don't worry about the bags, I'll unpack when I get home. Love you. Call you later."

"But..." Tobin kissed his disappointed husband and left. Victor exhaled and shook his head. "It's our last day."

Carbine City was in full motion. Its circuitry sang loudly. Citizens commuted. Advertisements protruded from businesses. Vehicles gave off steam in their haste. Police and Agents patrolled the streets.

The city's museum was alive as well, with viewers walking around taking in historical sights. The exhibits were full of artifacts from the olden days. Most electronics were still physical. Vehicles ran on gasoline. A more rustic time. People came in looking at older model cars and their engines. The tools either ran on gas or they were plugged in. Children and adults both fascinated by the olden days. Suddenly, a loud *crash*.

Distant screams echoed from beyond the hall of kitchen appliances, coming closer like a wave. They rushed in screaming. The bellow of a battle cry drowned out the commotion. While some of them fled, the others weren't so lucky.

Two men were thrown into the crowd.

WarMother stomped in after them, large and armored wearing a Viking helmet with cannons.

"I'd like to speak to the manager." She snarled.

Those trapped by the mad woman panicked. She paced eyeing the exhibits and the people.

The windows blew in as Agent Phoenix swung in on a cable. He landed and pulled his pistol.

"WarMother...Welcome to Carbine City."

ABOUT THE AUTHOR

Christopher Michael Carter currently resides in Missouri with his wife and daughter. He lives with Multiple Sclerosis and is hard at work on his next projects. You can find out more about Carter at BeavertownProductions.Blogspot.Com and you can find him on Twitter at @CMC5384. He can also be found on Instagram.

More from Christopher Michael Carter

<u>Fiction</u>
Last Rites of the Capacitance
Blue Sweep

<u>Poetry</u>
Gun Control for Polar Bears
Reflections at Various Speeds
Loose Lipped Secrets and Twinkling Lights

<u>Collections</u>
Sharp Items & Bad Intentions
Beyond the Wall
Duo de Macabre
How to Sell Sunblock to a Vampire

<u>Plays</u>
Doomsday Think Tank

www.ingramcontent.com/pod-product-compliance
Lightning Source LLC
Chambersburg PA
CBHW071820190726
48292CB00005B/1534